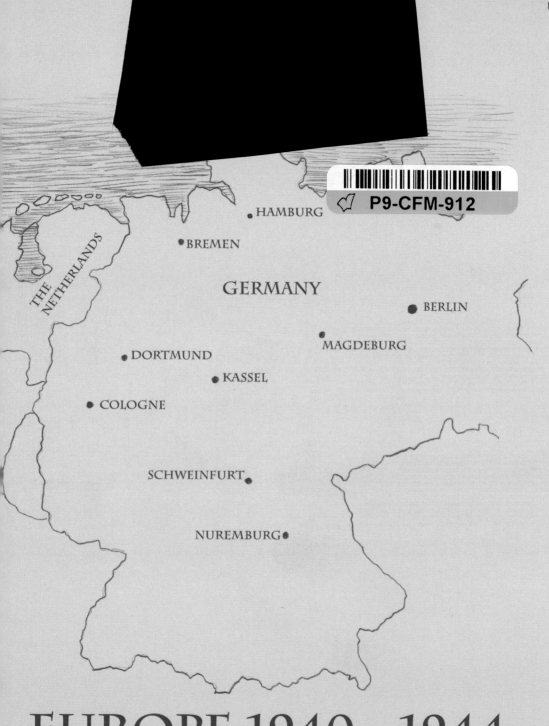

THE NETHERLANDS

•HAMBURG

•BREMEN

GERMANY

•BERLIN

•MAGDEBURG

•DORTMUND

•KASSEL

•COLOGNE

SCHWEINFURT•

NUREMBURG•

EUROPE 1940 – 1944

David
Mighty Eighth

BRIGHT SKY PRESS

Box 416
Albany, Texas 76430

Text copyright © 2007 by Marjorie Hodgson Parker
Illustrations copyright © 2007 by Mark Postlethwaite

10   9   8   7   6   5   4   3   2   1

Library of Congress Cataloging-in-Publication Data

Parker, Marjorie Hodgson.
    David and the Mighty Eighth : a British boy and a Texas airman in World War II / by Marjorie Hodgson Parker ; illustrated by Mark Postlethwaite.
        p. cm.
    ISBN 978-1-931721-93-6 (jacketed hardcover : alk. paper) 1. World War, 1939–1945—Great Britain—Juvenile fiction. 2. World War, 1939–1945—Evacuation of civilians—Great Britain—Juvenile fiction. [1. World War, 1939–1945—Evacuation of civilians—Great Britain—Fiction. 2. Friendship—Fiction. 3. United States. Army Air Forces. Air Force, 8th—Fiction. 4. World War, 1939–1945—Great Britain—Fiction.] I. Postlethwaite, Mark, 1964– ill. II. Title. III. Title: British boy and a Texas airman in World War II.

PZ7.P2272Dav 2007
[Fic]—dc22

2007025999

Book and cover design by Isabel Lasater Hernandez
Edited by Dixie Nixon

Printed in China through Asia Pacific Offset

David & the Mighty Eighth

Marjorie Hodgson Parker

Illustrated by Mark Postlethwaite

Foreword by E.G. "Buck" Shuler, Jr., Lt. General, USAF, Retired
Former Commander of the Eighth Air Force

Dedicated to:

David Hastings, the late Roger Freeman, the Eighth Air Force and all who have sacrificed and fought for freedom.

With many thanks to:

David and Jean Hastings, Jean and Roger Freeman, Vivian Rogers-Price and the Mighty Eighth Museum staff, Gen. E.G. "Buck" Shuler, Jr., "Hap" Chandler, Alfred Jenner, Maurice McCall, Mike Spiller, Joyce Wellham Coats Toth, Margaret and Douglas Wicker, Nelsie Chumlea, Cdr. Hamilton McWhorter, Pat Templer, Janet Stegeman, John Russell Thomasson; my young "editors," Austin Langemeier, Caleb and Caroline Hodgson, Carol, Christopher and Alisha Hart, Weston, Abigail, Leah and Gareb Jackson.

And with special thanks and love to my great supporter and husband, Joe, and to Marion Hodgson, my wonderful mother and untiring editor, who made this book possible.

FOREWORD

My interest in military aviation and history began during the traumatic days of World War II, when the story line of this wonderful book was unfolding in England. As a young lad growing up in South Carolina during the war—like David and Roger, the young characters in this poignant story—I was old enough to grasp the significant seriousness of the war. While my dad was serving in the Pacific as a naval officer, my family was out of harm's way having only to contend with "blackouts," rationing and other civil privations of war. But David and Roger and their families in England were enduring the direct attacks by the Luftwaffe from Nazi Germany.

Marjorie Parker has succeeded brilliantly in capturing the war's impact on these youngsters and their families as well as relating the magnificent Royal Air Force victory during the Battle of Britain and the decisive contributions of the mighty armada of the Eighth Air Force in achieving victory in the European Theater. This is an emotionally moving story that will enlighten all readers, but especially young readers, about hardship, sacrifice and the important events of World War II.

David and The Mighty Eighth is particularly meaningful to me, because I was privileged to know the two people upon whose lives the story is based. Reading this well-crafted story brought back many fond memories of my youth. I am honored to have been asked to pen this foreword and to endorse this remarkable book. I extend my sincerest appreciation to the author, Marjorie Hodgson Parker, for this singular honor.

E.G. "Buck" Shuler, Jr.
Lt. General, USAF, Retired
Former Commander of Eighth Air Force

INTRODUCTION

World War II began in September 1939, when Germany's dictator, Adolf Hitler, began sending his powerful military to take over Europe. Germany quickly crushed country after country. By June 1940, Great Britain stood alone against Hitler.

To be able to invade southern England, Hitler knew he would have to defeat Britain's Royal Air Force (RAF). So he sent his German air force, the Luftwaffe, across the English Channel to attack RAF bases. The result was the Battle of Britain, which began in July 1940, and was the first battle in history to control the air. By September, mistakenly thinking he had destroyed the RAF, Hitler sent the Luftwaffe to bomb London and other civilian targets. Their goal was to break the spirit of the people and force Britain to surrender. Air raids known as the Blitz took place nearly every night through the fall and winter.

And that's where our story begins…

CHAPTER 1

1940

Sirens wailed between deafening explosions. David slid under a metal bunk in the underground shelter. He lay facedown beside his mother in the dark dampness, his heart pounding. His older sister, Mary, lay under another bunk. In the dim flicker of the oil lamp, he saw friends and neighbors crowded closely, lying in almost every inch of space. The shelter, a deep trench covered with wooden beams, corrugated sheets of iron and earth, shuddered with each blast. David could feel his mother trembling. He hoped she wouldn't feel his shaking, too, as he laid an arm protectively over her. "You're the man of the house now," his dad had said as he left for the war. David wasn't sure how to be a man.

He squeezed his eyes shut and began counting the explosions. It helped distract him from his fear that a direct hit would kill them all. He remembered the warning Prime Minister Winston Churchill had given them before this Battle of Britain began: "The whole fury and might of the enemy must very soon be turned on us...." The earth shook with that fury now.

His mother began humming a little tune, as if it would help. David recognized it. "Whistle while you work. Hitler is a twerp. Goering's barmy, so's his army, whistle while you work."

They'd first sung that tune as they dug up their lawn and planted a vegetable garden. "Digging for victory," they had called it. David had liked the smell of the earth then. And he'd felt hopeful, planting the little seeds. But now the earthy smell of the shelter was one he hated, because it meant he'd spend another dreadful night jammed in with neighbors, uncomfortable and afraid. David knew thousands of others were in the tunnels of London's subway system, the Underground. It had become a bomb shelter, too, during this German Blitz of nighttime bombing raids.

He put his mouth close to his mother's ear. "Mum, do you think Dad is up there?"

He knew that his father, a Royal Air Force fighter pilot, was somewhere in the London area. Like every able-bodied man who could, his dad was fighting for Britain's survival against the enemy, Hitler's Nazis. From the time of Germany's first assault, his dad had defended England in his Spitfire, with eight machine guns in its wings. In that attack, 300 German bombers and 600 escorting fighters had descended upon them. The brave Royal Air Force had put up an incredible fight. They were heroes to all of Britain. To David, his dad was already a hero, long before the war. He hoped to be just like him. But right now, he didn't feel the least bit brave.

"I don't know where he is, love," his mother answered with a catch in her throat. "Say a prayer for him."

"I say lots of them," he said. He prayed his nightmares would never come true—nightmares of being outdoors watching dogfights in the sky, seeing his dad's olive and brown Spitfire take a direct hit, burst into flames and plummet toward the ground. He woke up from those dreams sweating and shivering at the same time. The dreams were almost as bad as the bombs. Another blast hit nearby, and David flinched.

Voices in the shelter cried out to God. Others cursed Hitler.

David wanted to curse Hitler, too. He gritted his teeth.

At last the explosions became distant rumbles. People began moving about cautiously, getting more comfortable until the next wave of bombs. Some children brought out playing cards. David, Mary and their mother stretched.

"We should try to get some sleep," their mother said. She turned to Mary, smoothing a strand of hair from her daughter's face. In the daytime, Mary's shining brown hair was combed neatly around her pretty face. Not tonight.

"I wish I could sleep," Mary said. "If only I could." With a frustrated sigh, she flopped down on her blanket, which was folded across the hard steel bunk. David could tell these weeks of all-night bombings were taking their toll on his sister. She never smiled anymore. She'd lost weight, looked pale, and startled easily.

Their mother squeezed into the bunk beside Mary, and David lay on the floor next to them. He watched two old men playing cards. One of them had on a lapel button that said, "Don't tell me; I've got a bomb story, too."

David wished he could laugh at that one. He wanted to laugh about something, anything. Instead, it seemed as though the shadowed darkness of the shelter had entered his soul. He was terrified for his father. In the war reports on the radio, BBC newsmen talked proudly about the brave battles being fought by outnumbered Royal Air Force pilots. For every RAF pilot shot down, they took down twice as many Germans. But David knew the Brits couldn't hold on forever. Their airfields had been bombed, their radar damaged, many of their planes destroyed and pilots killed. They needed help. And soon!

David wanted to help somehow—really help. He'd rather have been shooting than taking cover.

"David," his mother said quietly, leaning down from the bed, "we've talked about this before, but now I'm sure. I'm going to have to send you and Mary to the country for protection. I'm worried about Mary. I need you to help take care of her and go with her to Nana and Grandfather's."

"But, Mum, what about you? You must come too," he said. He didn't want her to stay and face this alone. Besides, he and Mary needed her, too. They'd never been alone before with Grandfather, a tight-jawed, strict disciplinarian. It would be bad enough without his dad's hearty laugh to offset his grandfather's sternness. What would it be like without even Mum?

"I can't leave my job," his mother said. "The factory needs all its workers. When I inspect the radios, I like to think I'm helping your father. Sometimes I find a loose wire or something that could jar loose during combat. When I fix it, I've helped him or one of our other pilots; they need good radios in their planes. Besides, if your father gets any time off to come home, I want to be here. I know you will miss that, but he wants you with his parents. He shouldn't have to worry about anything other than fighting."

"And you."

"Yes. And me," she said with a half smile.

"Well," David said with determination, "at least if I

go to the country I can finally do something that matters like you do. I'll work the farm with Grandfather. I'll be part of the Land Army that feeds England." He knew Germany was trying to starve England out of the war by sinking the merchant ships that brought much of England's food from abroad. German submarines called U-Boats were succeeding in sinking many cargo ships, and food was in short supply. England's farmers were planting more crops to feed their hungry nation.

Secretly, David wondered if his grandfather would trust him with anything important on the farm. He didn't know the first thing about farming. And he never felt he measured up to Grandfather's expectations about anything else.

"Don't forget, school comes first," his mother cautioned. "But after your school work, I know your grandfather would be very happy to have your help. He's lost all his farmhands to the war. He needs both you and Mary."

When the all-clear signal sounded the next morning, they trudged out of the stuffy shelter, stiff and tired. The coolness of the outdoor air felt good, but it was dusty and smoke-filled. David coughed. Blinking against the sunlight, he stared at incredible destruction—homes and buildings turned to rubble, fires raging everywhere. Emergency workers and neighbors rushed around to help the injured. Homeless children wept on the curb. David turned to look at Mary. She gazed around with a vacant expression, her wide-set green eyes reddened and dull.

He knew he and Mary would have to honor their parents' wishes and leave London. But how could he leave his Mum, his friends, his home? The thought of it gave him an empty, lonely feeling. He knew many of the neighbors' children already had been evacuated to various places in the country where they'd be safe from the Blitz. Many even went to live with strangers. People with spare rooms had been ordered by the government to open up their homes to young evacuees. In desperation, some parents had even sent their children across the ocean to the United States and Canada to live with host families there.

David knew he and Mary, with their own family to go

to, were luckier than most. So he should be glad, he told himself. After all, he liked the big farm near the city of Norwich. And on holidays with his family there, he'd always felt the adoration of his tender Nana.

Thinking about her now, he could almost taste the warm, freshly-baked apple pie she made. But he knew he wouldn't get any pie with the war going on. Rationing limited the amount of sugar, as well as foods and other goods allowed each family. Special treats were out of the question. Life on the farm wouldn't be as he remembered. But nothing was the same anymore.

David felt changed, too. The war had forced him to grow up quickly. But he'd have to prove that to Grandfather. He would learn to shoot a gun and hunt. He'd work hard and show enough responsibility to drive the farm machinery. Surely he could win Grandfather's approval.

But what would it be like, living under Grandfather's strict rule? How long would he have to live away from his parents? What would a new school be like where he knew no one? A little knot formed in his stomach.

CHAPTER 2

T he bomb-damaged Liverpool Street Railway Station in London was noisy with activity when the three of them arrived on a chilly, gray morning. David and Mary set their suitcases down on the platform as their mother bought their train tickets to Norwich. He watched many small children waiting, too, dolls and stuffed animals clutched to their chests, large identity labels pinned to their clothing. Their cardboard gas mask boxes hung around their necks. David thought they looked frightened. He wondered how many of them would rather face bombs than life without their parents.

Holding a small boy about two, a worried-looking woman ran up to David and Mary. The sleepy child looked lost in a wooly cardigan twice his size.

"Where are you going?" she asked breathlessly.

"Norwich," David said.

"Could you take Bennie?" she pleaded. "Could you let him off at Ipswich? His aunt will pick him up." Then she leaned in toward David and whispered, "His parents were killed two nights ago."

David didn't know what to say. He looked toward Mary, who stood with her back to them.

"We could take him, couldn't we, Mary?" he asked. When Mary didn't turn around, David awkwardly held out his arms to take the chubby, curly-headed child. Bennie came to him without a fuss.

"Thank you. Bless you," the woman said. She handed David instructions, a ticket, and a paper sack along with a coupon book of ration stamps to purchase the limited food and clothing allowed one person. "Be a good boy, Bennie." She kissed him, and then disappeared through the sea of people on the platform.

"Who was that?" David's mother asked, walking up. "And who is this?" She touched the child's soft, fat cheek and smiled.

"Some lady. And this is Bennie. We're taking him as far as Ipswich."

Mary turned and seemed to come out of her daze. "May I hold him?"

David gave her the sleepy child.

David and his mother smiled at each other. It was the first thing Mary had said since last night.

"Here are your tickets, some jam tarts and lemonade," his mother said. Suddenly she looked very sad. David felt a lump aching in his throat. "I don't want to let you go," his mother said, "but I want you to be safer. All of England is dangerous, but right now London is the worst. Nana and Grandfather have their own shelter in the country, you know. And since they're outside of Norwich, it won't be as bad as it is in the city. I'll write you. Keep your chin up. Say your prayers. And remember that I love you." Her last words were choked. She kissed David and held him a long time. David tried hard to swallow the lump, but it just hurt worse as he put his arms around his mother.

She turned to Mary, who seemed comforted by the quiet child in her arms. "Mary, love, you will finally get some rest. Please take care of yourself. I know Nana will enjoy all the help you can give her. Just think, next week, you'll be 14! I'll be singing to you in my heart on your birthday."

"Mum. I'm afraid for you. Please come with us," Mary said.

"We'll be together again before you know it," her mother answered. "I love you, Mary." Bennie was caught between them in their embrace.

The guard blew his whistle. Children were urged aboard. They waved from every window, some smiling, some crying. David and Mary heaved their bags from the platform and climbed aboard with Bennie. David blew a last kiss to his mother. The train whistle blew, and with great, loud blasts of steam, the engine began chugging out. David's heart wanted to break.

CHAPTER 3

February 1942

David had been relieved when the Blitz against London had finally ended in May 1941. The eight months of bombing had failed in its purpose—to break the will of the British to fight. Britain had been saved for the time being by the gallant "few" of RAF Fighter Command—and his dad was one of them.

The war still raged, and bombs exploded all over England, but not with the intensity of the Blitz. It had been 16 months since David and Mary had placed Bennie in his aunt's arms at Ipswich and then stepped off the train themselves in Norwich. And they'd felt safer. Even though Norwich was the target of hit-and-run raids two or three times a week, it was much less dangerous than London. Their mother had urged them to stay on at the farm even when the Blitz ended.

At their grandparents' home, they had their own Anderson bomb shelter in the garden just 30 yards from the back door. And the five miles that stretched between them and Norwich lessened the chance of their being bombed. Besides that, their two-storied, thatched-roof farmhouse, built by their great-grandfather, wasn't a likely target. It stood alone, surrounded by fields, apple and pear trees. The Luftwaffe's mission was to destroy cities, their factories and the people in them, not lone farmhouses, though they sometimes did that, too.

Their first weeks at Nana and Grandfather's, Mary had slept almost constantly. Now she had blossomed again. The broad smile that dimpled both cheeks had returned. Her green eyes, set off by heavy, dark lashes, danced with life once more. She helped on the farm along with David, and the outdoors had given her a healthy glow. Still slender, she'd developed some womanly curves, too, and David was amused to watch men's heads turn when she walked down the lane with him.

During these months on the farm, David had noticed his own looks changing, as well. His dark hair had lightened in the sun, his fair skin had tanned, and a few freckles had appeared across his nose. Even though he was still slim, he was thicker across the shoulders, and his arms muscled from the hard work. Learning farm chores had come easily to him—much more easily than school work. He still struggled with that.

Now he sat at the kitchen table, books piled around him, trying to force himself to finish his homework. He liked this warm place near the kitchen stove where Mary and Nana were preparing dinner.

"How are maths and science coming?" Mary asked, cutting up potatoes.

"It's better now that Roger is helping." Roger was his new friend. "But, I wish it was as easy for me as it is for him." He paused. "We cycled to his house yesterday to study."

"Where does he live?"

"Near the school. He showed me the spot where two of his best friends used to live. There was nothing left there. During the Norwich Blitz, their house took a direct hit and they were killed. They didn't have time to get to a bomb shelter."

"I'm afraid we'd all got a bit too sure of ourselves," Nana said, shaking her head. "German bombers had always flown past Norwich on their way to more important targets...."

"Like London," Mary said sadly.

Nana nodded. "After awhile, even when air raid sirens sounded, most people around here stopped running to shelter. So we were taken by surprise when the Norwich Blitz began. The city was mostly undefended that first night, too." She slowly stirred the boiling soup pot as Mary dropped in some chunks of potato.

"What did you do?" David asked.

"Your grandfather and I had time to run to our shelter, but we didn't even grab a torch. Turns out we didn't need one. Night was like day. Bombs and fire bombs and parachute flares lit up everything, even here in the country."

"Roger told me his school room was blasted that same night. Even his books were destroyed," David said, closing one of his with a thump. "Bombs wouldn't be so bad if they were dropped only on books."

"David, you wouldn't want a world without books," Nana scolded him.

"Doesn't sound so bad to me," he retorted.

"Keep trying, David, you'll get it," Mary said with an encouraging smile.

"One day, you'll be glad you kept at it," Nana added.

"I like working on the farm better," he said. "There are no exams. Besides, I get a science lesson every day in nature. It's easier to understand than books."

He enjoyed planting and harvesting wheat, barley and sugar beets, helping Grandfather milk the cows and deliver fresh milk on the milk round. He liked caring for the animals and the garden and picking fruit from the trees. He enjoyed smelling honeysuckle and wild roses and gathering green clusters of elderberries for Nana's special jelly. He didn't even mind lifting the hay bales in summer. It seemed as if all school did was give him problems and get him into trouble—and with trouble at school came those awful canings.

"The more you study and learn, the better farmer you'll be," Nana said. "Besides, being good at figures will help you keep up with farm accounts."

David looked wearily at the stack of books. "I wish Dad were here. He could somehow make all this easier—I guess because he could make me laugh while he helped me with my homework."

In his letters, David's father often asked about his school work. David was amazed that his father could even think about that when he was fighting a war. David sighed. He had written to his dad that since he couldn't help him in the war, he would at least fight "the battle of the books." So he'd better get busy.

And he would, as soon as he wrote to his mum. He took out a piece of paper.

Dear Mum,

It's been three months since your last visit. When are you coming again? I wish Dad could get enough time off to come here, too. I miss you both.

I've carved some new model airplanes to show you. Since there are plenty of poplar trees around, I'm never short of wood. Glue and paint are hard to get, but in Norwich there's a great model shop on St. Benedicts Street. Mr. Williment, the owner, helps me all he can. Everyone seems to like my model Spitfires. I sold some to a toy shop. And I gave one to an auction where they were raising funds to buy a Spitfire for the RAF. My plane brought a good sum. Maybe someday Dad will fly in the new Spitfire that I helped to buy.

Twice a week, in Scouts, we collect scrap metal and paper. In between, we've been rebuilding the Scout hut that was bombed before Mary and I moved here. My friend Roger said the bombing came during school. The boys were outside playing cricket, and the Germans machine-gunned their playing field, too. All the fellows dived into a trench and muddied their white cricket clothes, but they weren't hurt. It's really scary to think that Hitler says he wants to destroy the world-wide Scout movement. I'm so glad Dad is helping protect us from that madman.

Mary and Nana have been stretching our rations with eggs from the chickens and vegetables from the winter garden. Nana is a good cook, but I am very tired of cabbage, parsnips and brussels sprouts. I miss the kind of food we had before the war. However, Grandfather has taught me to shoot. I killed a rabbit yesterday. Nana begged a bone from the butcher so she could boil it and skim the lard off the top. Then she made a pastry for a rabbit pie. It was the best *meal I've had since the war began, and it was my rabbit.*

Now that I'm 11, I'm growing fast. Nana measured me, and my marks on the kitchen doorframe exactly match Dad's when he was my age. I wrote to him that he'd better hurry home before I outgrow him. My trousers can't be let out any farther, so Nana has altered some of Grandfather's old clothes for me to wear. When we're milking together, I look rather like him.

Bombs fall on Norwich several times a week, and Roger and I have started collecting bomb fragments. I have quite a collection. Nana said she heard at the Red Cross that three houses had been hit last week. But don't worry about us. Every night I make sure the blackout curtains are drawn so that no chinks of light show from around them. When we milk in the dark, we're careful that no lantern light can be seen from the barn. If there's a full "bombers' moon," we stay ready to run to the shelter if the sirens sound. Even the cat, Dickens, runs there with us. I wish you were here, too.

Mum, come soon and stay for good. Love from us all.

As he signed his name, David felt a wave of homesickness. The war, the rationing of food and clothes and fuel, the blackness of nights, the separation from his parents and friends, he hated it all.

Homesickness was replaced by anger. How dare that devil Hitler think he had the right to take over Europe and destroy everything good? David had read of the terrible suffering of the people in the Nazi-occupied countries. Great Britain was the only country that hadn't surrendered. And she would not fall! David knew his countrymen would die to keep Great Britain free from that madman. And he would fight, too! He was anxious to show some real courage. But, even as he dreamed of being a fighter pilot, deep inside he wondered if he had what it took.

"Germany will run out of bombs before England runs out of courage," his grandfather had said.

"But courage doesn't prevent us from all being wiped out," David wanted to argue. He thought about little Bennie, who would grow up without his parents, and wondered how many other children would be orphaned by the war. Great Britain desperately needed help against her huge and powerful enemy, and David wondered how long they could hold on.

CHAPTER 4

1943

In the spring of 1942, David heard with great relief that American airmen had begun arriving at airfields in England. But the thrill of that news wasn't like the joy he felt now as he parked his bicycle beside the farmhouse. The Yanks were coming almost to his back door!

He and Roger had spent a fun day watching final construction work on the new airfield—*their* airfield, they called it—across the road from the house. For months, road graders, concrete mixers and heavy machinery had been transforming part of Grandfather's farm into an airfield. The government had taken 500 acres of his land to build on. Grandfather hadn't resented it. He'd been glad to help the war effort. Then, he had been hired to oversee the building of the airfield, Attlebridge, which he was qualified to do. Grandfather had said that perhaps by March, the American pilots would arrive at *their* field.

Runways now criss-crossed the muddy countryside. The field was encircled by a concrete track around the perimeter, with round concrete hardstands on which the planes would be parked. On the edge of the field were hangars, buildings, workshops and metal Nissen huts, which looked like giant tin cans buried on their sides. The Nissen huts served as barracks and offices. A two-story camouflaged control tower stood to one side.

David and Roger had spent much of their free time over the Christmas holidays watching Attlebridge's progress. Other airfields were being built all over East Anglia, their part of eastern England. Americans were already training and flying from some of the bases.

"Americans are coming, and we'll win this blasted war! The Nazis and their Luftwaffe won't cause trouble any more!" David had chanted as Roger laughed. He was still whistling the tune as he walked in the back door.

"Mum!" There she sat at the kitchen table. She jumped up as David rushed to greet her. "You've come! You didn't tell us! Can you stay this time?" They hugged hard and long.

"I'll stay," she said, but something wasn't right in the tone of her voice. He stood back from her and looked into her tired eyes.

"What's wrong, Mum?"

"Sit down, love." David's heart began to race. His knees felt wobbly. Dread stole over him. Where were Nana and Grandfather?

"You must be strong when I tell you this," his mother said, laying a hand over his. David could tell she was determined to be strong herself. "Your father is missing in action."

David couldn't breathe.

She continued, "His plane was shot down over Holland. He was seen parachuting out. He could have been picked up by the Dutch resistance fighters, the Underground. Or," she paused and took a deep breath, "he could be a prisoner of war."

David felt his eyes stinging. "But he's not dead?"

"We don't know that, but I refuse to think the worst. I want you to hope with me."

David bit his tongue deliberately so he wouldn't cry. Nana came into the kitchen, her face blotchy. She dabbed angrily at her eyes with the corner of her apron. Grandfather followed her. They walked toward David. Sun-baked lines in his grandfather's ruddy face suddenly seemed deeper, as if he had aged ten years.

When the three of them encircled him, and David felt Grandfather's arms around him for the first time ever, something gave way inside. He wept like a sissy. Like a girl. But he was powerless to stop the sobs; they just boiled up from deep within. It was as if all his unspoken anger and fear had combined with grief and exploded. Finally, he took some deep, ragged breaths and stopped crying. With burning eyes and wanting to vomit, he felt a strange numbness take over his mind.

He knew Mary would be home from the grocer's in a few minutes. He would have to pretend to be strong. They would all have to be strong for Mary.

CHAPTER 5

*H*e *was outdoors, watching a dogfight in the skies.... the Spitfire was hit and burst into flames.... it was diving out of control toward the ground.... and his dad! His father was outside the plane, falling, falling....*

David cried, "Dad!" but no sound came. He woke up. His heart pounded. His mind groped through the darkness for reality. It had been a nightmare. But, he realized as he fully awakened, it was true. His dad had been shot down. Heavy sadness descended on him again. He clenched his fists. If only he could fight those cursed Nazis!

He had no idea what time it was. His mother shared Mary's bed near him, and neither stirred. He listened to Mary's rhythmic breathing. The soft, almost purring sound was comforting. It was much better than the muffled sobs he'd heard the night before after they'd gone to bed. He whispered his ten-thousandth prayer for his father.

Even during the dark days of the Battle of Britain, the threat of invasion and the Blitz, David hadn't felt like this. He had had some hope. His father had been out there fighting to keep them safe. Now David didn't know where his dad was, or even if he were alive.

Rolling over and reaching out to pull back the blackout curtain, David felt as if his strength and courage had been blacked out by sadness. Would this bloody war never end? As the curtain parted, winter's chill seeped in from the cold window. Dim morning light glittered on the frost-covered farm fields.

Was it just yesterday he and Roger had stood out there, giddy with expectation?

David heard the machines in the field firing up again now. He felt the smallest flicker of hope struggling to return. The Yanks were coming! Perhaps now they could win this war and his father, if he were alive, would be rescued. If they could win the war, the awful fear and suffering would stop. His father would return, and with his hearty laugh, scoop them all into his strong arms.

"David," his mother whispered.

"Morning, Mum," he said. He left the curtain partially open to let some light in. Rolling over, he faced her.

"Did you sleep?"

"Some," he answered. "You?"

"A bit." Her head was cradled on a thin arm. Those same dark circles under her brown eyes that had been there all through the war made her look older than 37. Yet, no matter what, her eyes had sparkled. Before the war it had been a mischievous twinkle. As the war dragged on, it was more like stubborn, fiery resolve.

He desperately searched her eyes now for a glimpse of that gleam. Did she really have hope? If he could just see a glimmer of it there, then maybe he could hope, too.

"Happy birthday," she said, smiling. "My New Year's Eve baby is just a year away from being a teenager."

David saw a hint of the old sparkle return.

"My birthday … I'd forgotten," he said. If his father had been home, and if there weren't rationing, today they would have had roast beef with Yorkshire pudding and horseradish sauce. They would have ended the day with fruity, iced birthday cake, seeing in the New Year and pretending all the world was celebrating David's birthday. If his father was out there, did he know what day it was?

Mary stirred. She always slept half buried in her sheets and blankets, with only the crown of her thick dark hair showing. She pulled the sheets off her face, and David saw it was swollen from crying.

"It is your day," she said sleepily, with a sort of hollowness to her voice. "We'll have to make a sweet for you."

David heard Nana putting the kettle on in the kitchen. He was surprised Grandfather had let him sleep instead of getting him up for milking. He'd never known Grandfather to allow any variation in their daily farm routine. He didn't think he was getting special treatment for his birthday. Grandfather just knew it had been a long, bad night.

"I'd better go help Grandfather," he said, getting up and wincing as his bare feet met the cold stone floor. In the chill, he quickly pulled on his trousers, which were getting short, and the sweater his grandmother had knitted.

David was glad to have a job to do. Especially now. It might not win the war, but it was necessary to keep England fed. He usually didn't mind having Grandfather's work-roughened hand shaking his shoulder at 4:30 a.m. to wake him. He didn't even much mind Grandfather barking orders at him like a sergeant, now that he was used to it.

He brushed his teeth and splashed icy water on his face. Perhaps Grandfather acted like a sergeant because he had been one in the last war, the Great War, World War I. He'd been shot in the leg and still limped from it. But it didn't slow him down. It just made him grumpy.

"I'd fight again, if they'd take me," he'd said.

David believed it. Even at age 59, Grandfather was strong and energetic. His shoulders were broad, his large hands thick with muscle from milking, and his arms powerful. Only a sprinkling of silver in his dark hair showed his advancing years. It seemed he could do anything. With his construction skills, he'd tackled the government job of overseeing building the airfield on his acreage. David and Mary had taken over more farm chores to ease Grandfather's load. Still, he found time to work with them and, like a strict inspector, was forever checking behind them. David heard many stern lectures on how to improve. All last year, from before daylight to dark, it seemed to David that Grandfather had done the job of two men. Then he'd spent several hours on Home Guard duty at night.

David had gone with him only a few times on his Home Guard duty. On a tall hill on Eaton Golf Course overlooking the river Yare, Grandfather and other older volunteers watched over the countryside. David was horrified to see that Grandfather's gun was the only one the group on duty had. The others carried pitchforks and pickaxe handles. But, if German paratroopers ever landed, David knew the Guard would fight them with whatever they had, and Grandfather would most likely lead the charge. A huge hydrogen-filled barrage balloon was also based on the golf course and flew over them at 3,000 feet, attached by a cable to an RAF winch lorry on the ground. Many barrage ballons floated over Norwich, their cables helping protect the city from low-flying German planes.

Now as David pulled on his socks, an old pair of resoled rubber boots, and his heavy jacket, he wondered how Grandfather would act this morning. He knew neither his grandfather nor grandmother would talk about their feelings. Nana's eyes might still be rimmed with red, but she would wear a brave smile on her sweet, round face. When they came in from milking, she'd serve them their standard breakfast: porridge oats with fresh milk. If there was any tea, they'd have a steaming cup. Then, she'd leave, as usual, for her work with the Red Cross. As a nurse and deputy commandant of the Norwich group, she had many responsibilities.

Grandfather would relieve his distress with hard work, holding his feelings inside. David wished they could talk. But he dared not share his fears with Grandfather. He would probably say something like, "Stop it at once, and be British!" To Grandfather, being British was synonymous with self-control and courage.

Yanking a wool cap over his ears, David slipped out the back door into the cold.

As he passed the winter garden and the water well, he heard the unmilked cows in the barn bawling impatiently. The heavy barn door creaked as he opened it. Grandfather sat perched on a milking stool with the tortoiseshell cat Dickens sitting attentively close by, waiting for a squirt. The streams of milk made rhythmic milk bucket music. While continuing to milk, Grandfather turned his head toward David.

"Mornin'," he said. "I thought you were going to sleep the day away. Better get busy—the girls are irritated." Then he added, "Happy birthday, lad!"

"Thanks, Grandfather," David said. He noticed the dark circles under his grandfather's eyes. Hay on the barn floor felt cushiony under his rubber boots as he walked to the next stall. The pungent barn smells were comforting. He scooped some cattle cake into a bucket for the cow to munch on when he milked her. Blowing on his fingers to warm them, he sat down to milk.

"Grandfather, was World War I as bad as this one?" he asked, gently rubbing the cow's side in greeting.

"All war is bad," he answered. "We thought World War I was the war to end all wars. But we underestimated the bitterness of the people we beat. Their desire for revenge started this war."

"Well, in six years, I'll be old enough to be a pilot," David said. "If we win the war."

"Not *if*," his grandfather interrupted. "We *will* win the war, no ifs about it."

"*When* we win the war," David said, and it felt good to say it. "When we win the war, I'm going to fly for the RAF and help make Britain so strong that no one will dare attack us ever again."

"If you want to be a pilot, you'd better work harder in school," Grandfather said.

"I'm trying," David said, defensively. Grandfather was always on his back about his exams. "I just can't...."

"Don't use the word can't," Grandfather interrupted. "You can! Just set your mind to it. Just like this war. We will win. Never give up. Nothing worth having is easy."

David wanted to retort, "It's easy for Roger," but he knew better than to act cheeky with his grandfather. He kept milking, laying his forehead against the cow's side, feeling empty.

By the time they finished, David was eager to warm himself beside the kitchen stove. He walked side by side with Grandfather back to the house, matching steps with him. Grandfather's limp was more noticeable on cold mornings.

David remembered how when his father walked with him, he always laid an arm on David's shoulder. He wished Grandfather would do that. It wouldn't be the same as walking with his dad, but it would help. He wondered if Grandfather ever showed affection like that.

Removing his boots by the door, David heard the women's voices in the kitchen. It sounded like any other morning.

Yes, David thought, with stiff resolve, each of them would carry on. They would do their work, help others, sacrifice for the war effort. And each night, they would ask for God's help and protection.

Today, they'd celebrate David's birthday, mixing precious rations of sugar, eggs, flour and fruit and forming them into rocky heaps, baking a "rock cake."

He knew there could be no icing. Tomorrow, they would go to the Saturday night village dance and cheer up the RAF "flyboys" at the nearby bases. Sunday morning, they would go to church. They would begin the New Year of 1944 with hope.

"We shall never surrender," Prime Minister Winston Churchill had said. They wouldn't. His countrymen would not surrender to the enemy or to fear or to despair. Even if it cost them their lives ...

C H A P T E R 6

January 1944

The school day dragged for David. He'd been paying closer attention and studying harder since resolving to become a pilot, but today he couldn't concentrate. At lunch, he could hear more about the news that had been whispered among his friends that morning: The Americans in the Eighth Air Force were coming any day to Horsham St. Faith airfield, an old RAF base which wasn't far from school. David heard a distant rumbling. Bombers? Now that American airfields had been built, were the Germans striking again? The drone became louder, closer. Vibrations sent tremors through his body. He waited for air raid sirens, but they didn't sound. It wasn't Germans. It was the Yanks!

Suddenly, every chair in the classroom scraped back, as boys scrambled to the window. David was one of the first searching the cold blue sky and seeing what he'd hoped for. Roger stood next to him, watching wave after wave of huge, low-flying, four-engine bombers. Even the teacher stood at the window, staring in awe.

David and Roger looked at each other and grinned. "Aviation mad" his mother called them. They were. It's all they talked about over honey sandwiches at lunch. They'd even planned to play truant to watch the planes. Though it would mean a caning from the headmaster, it would be worth it. Since he and Roger didn't live at the school, their punishment wouldn't carry over to unpleasant duties in the school house where the others boarded.

"All right, boys," the teacher said after a few minutes. "Time for lunch."

Escape time. It was easy to sneak away, while the teachers were distracted. David and Roger grabbed their coats, jumped on their bicycles, and rode hard to the airfield. David was glad the snow had melted off the road.

"Look at 'em," David cried, craning his neck and almost falling off his bike. More four-engine Liberators

came in to land. They were as huge as their shadows. Their powerful engines' roar was deafening.

Cycling up to the main gate, Roger and David hid behind the hedgerow. David knew he would never be able to play truant like this when the planes arrived at *his* airfield, Attlebridge. It was too close to home, and he'd be caught for sure. But here at Horsham St. Faith, he was miles away from the farm. Still, David felt fearful Grandfather might spot him somehow.

The main gate was as close as they could come to the field, because all the old RAF bases had high wire fences around them. He was glad the newly-built American bases weren't that way. People could get close to them. And if any Yanks ever invited them to have a look, David knew he and Roger could vault the low fence.

Now he would have to be content gawking from the main gate. They watched their first real Americans swinging down out of the planes and walking off together, laughing and talking.

"They sound just like the cinema," Roger said.

Sometime after the planes landed, David punched Roger in the arm.

"Look, some chaps are coming to the gate!"

A group of men in uniform walked straight toward them, heading out the main gate. David felt like snapping to attention.

"Hi, boys," one airman drawled.

"Hullo." David's heart was thumping hard.

The airman reached in his pocket and took out something. "Wish I had some candy for you kids," he said. "But here's a souvenir from America." With a wink, he reached toward David and pressed two silver coins in his hand.

"Thank you, sir," he cried, as the men walked away. David turned to Roger. "Look! American money! One for each of us!"

They turned the coins over in their hands, studying them.

"Twenty-five cent pieces. I like the Yanks already." Roger smiled. David carefully pocketed his treasure and turned again to look at the airfield.

"Look at those planes! And the pictures on them," David said. "Wow. This is a lot more interesting than anatomy class." They stared at the naked and half-clothed girls painted on the noses of the planes. "We could tell the headmaster we were out getting an education." He chuckled.

"And making money," Roger added.

David read some of the names painted beside the figures: *Dixie Belle, Dream Boat, Totin' Mama.*

"Uh, oh!" Roger said, pointing. A man wearing a military police uniform, a gun strapped at his side, stalked toward them.

David thought the man looked awfully tough and unfriendly. "That's one Yank I don't want to meet," David said. "Let's get out of here!" They scrambled to their bikes and took off.

David couldn't wait to talk to his family about the planes and the Americans. But he would have to hide the quarter. And he mustn't slip up and say anything that let them know he'd played truant.

That night in bed, as he shivered under the covers waiting for the wrapped hot brick from the oven to warm him, he reflected on his day. He tried to focus on the fun of telling his friends about it, pushing aside the dread of the caning that would await him at school.

C H A P T E R   7

The next morning at school, David waited for Roger.

As Roger parked his bicycle, David asked, "Did your family find out?"

"Everyone was so excited, no one asked how I'd seen so much," he said grinning. "My mother said the noise of the fly-over had rattled the chimney pots."

"If my Grandfather finds out, I'm afraid he'll rattle *me!*" David said. "I'm glad we don't have a phone, and I hope the headmaster doesn't write my family...." His voice trailed off as the headmaster suddenly materialized, his tall, rigid figure framed in the school doorway.

Mr. Hetherington's glasses were perched on the end of his long nose. His slightly bulging eyes glared at the boys. "Meet me in my study," he ordered as David and

Roger walked in.

He followed behind them as if escorting prisoners to the gallows.

"Stop cracking your knuckles, Freeman," Mr. Hetherington said as he picked up the long, thin cane from behind his huge desk.

First came the lecture, then the caning for playing truant. As he leaned over the desk, David concentrated on yesterday's fun instead of the pain.

"It could have been worse," Roger said afterward as they walked to class.

"If Grandfather finds out, it *will* be worse," David said, still worrying. "If I sit down too gently at tea, he'll suspect something. But, never mind. It was worth it. Yesterday's the first time I've felt really happy since my father went down."

From then on, they waited until after school to go out to the airfield. They lived for Saturday, when a gang of friends rode out with them and they could spend the day. David was glad it was winter, because there were fewer farm chores. He didn't mind the cold so much, but he was sorry the days were short. Once they cycled 20 miles to look at the planes at different fields, and David barely got home in time to milk. He could have been in serious trouble. He decided not to ride so far next time.

Having a big group of friends to ride with reminded David of his days in London as part of the "pram squad." He and other school boys had taken baby carriages and gathered wood from destroyed buildings to use for fires for heat. Perhaps this wasn't as helpful, but it was much more fun.

Most days, only three of them went to the airfields: David, Roger and Roger's cousin, Mac, who was three years younger. Mac was small and skinny, a bundle of energy. A tuft of his dark hair stuck up in front no matter how much he combed it. David wondered if his hair grew like that because Mac was always in motion. He could pedal fast and talk even faster.

Mac seemed the opposite of his cousin. Roger was tall, wore glasses and a serious expression that David thought made him look grown up. When they were having fun, though, Roger's solemn look was banished by his wide smile.

One afternoon, Mac announced breathlessly, "I heard you can get close to the planes at Rackheath. Let's ride out there."

They took off down the road, turning onto Green Lane West, the main road of the village that ran right through the base.

"It would be fun to live here," David said. "I've never seen an airfield almost inside a village."

When they arrived, they hung over the fence, looking at the wide-tailed B-24 Liberators of the 2nd Air Division of the Eighth Air Force.

"The ground crew might be friendly," David said, hopefully. "They don't look awfully much older than we are."

One of the Americans saw them. "Hey, fellows! Want a look?" he called.

"Yes sir." The three of them jumped the fence and ran toward the planes.

"Any of you got an older sister?" one of the mechanics asked.

Mac spoke before David could. "I've got three."

The Yank hoisted him into the plane.

"I've got one, too," David said.

"When he's had a look, you can get into the cockpit," the American said. "Want some candy?"

He took out a Hershey bar and divided it between David and Roger.

"Chocolate! Wow! Thanks." David had never seen a Hershey bar, and it had been years since he'd had chocolate. While he waited his turn to climb into the plane, David ate it slowly, letting the sweetness melt in his mouth.

"Uh, oh. MPs," the mechanic said. "Come on out, kid!" he called to Mac. Mac appeared, and the mechanic helped him down and shooed them away.

"Bring your sisters by sometime," he shouted after them as they ran off.

Mac was so excited that David could hardly understand a word he said about the cockpit. He wasn't sure he even wanted to hear, because he was so disappointed he'd missed his chance to climb in.

"If I could turn my little brother into a girl, I would." Roger complained.

As they sped home, David wondered why the Yanks

even thought about girls when they had airplanes to work on and fly. But, if it took a girl to impress them, he'd have to figure out a way to talk Mary into coming with him sometime. He began to plot.

C H A P T E R   8

March 1944

In the spring, the Yanks finally arrived at Attlebridge, *his* airfield, and David loved the amazing change in country life. Now, before dawn, the exciting roar of airplane engines drowned out nature's sounds. Planes took off and circled, waiting for others to join the formation. He'd heard that as many as 1,000 Liberators formed up, then flew off. On a clear day, vapor trails from the planes lined the blue sky like chalk marks.

The sound of planes was almost constant now and was fondly called "the sound of freedom." Active airfields were located almost every eight miles in David's area of East Anglia, near the English Channel. It was jokingly called the Aircraft Carrier of Great Britain.

From their own bases farther north, the RAF planes—Lancasters, Halifaxes, Stirlings, and a few older Wellingtons—took off at sunset in a continuous stream of ones and twos for their nighttime bombing raids against Germany. On their way, the planes flew low over the Norfolk countryside to avoid enemy radar. They returned around 3:00 a.m., some days at dawn. The Americans took off just before dawn for daylight precision bombing and returned five to eight hours later.

David no longer needed Grandfather's copy of *Aeroplane Spotter* magazine to recognize planes. He not only could identify all the aircraft, but he could tell by the sound of the engines which planes were flying over. The Allies intended to bring Germany to its knees with round-the-clock raids on factories, air bases and cities.

At first, the constant takeoffs and landings had made the cows nervous. Now they seemed accustomed to it. But it still bothered Mary. The noise brought back her nightmares about the Blitz.

"I wish for my 18th birthday tomorrow that the Yanks and the RAF would take a holiday," she said. "And we could have peace and quiet for just one day."

Sure enough, the next morning, a miserable drizzly fog crept in, and Mary got her wish. Planes were grounded.

That day, as David dressed for school, his mother left as usual on her bicycle for her factory job in Norwich. This time, Mary rode along with her on Grandfather's old bicycle so that she could register for war work at the Labour Exchange. It was a requirement for everyone at age 18. Since she'd been working on Grandfather's farm for three years, Mary would not be required to do industry work. She had confided to David that she'd been tempted to volunteer for the Women's Auxiliary Air Force as a WAAF, but had changed her mind when she realized how much Grandfather needed them on the farm. So now, officially, she was labeled a "Land Girl" in the Women's Land Army.

That night, as they celebrated Mary's birthday over dinner, David's mother smiled across the table at her family. "I'm the only factory worker in a Land Army family," she said. "I still don't know how to milk a cow or operate a farm, but I've found a way to make some extra money from home. A friend told me an American chaplain at Hethel airfield needs someone to do his laundry. I haven't met him, but I signed up!"

She turned to David. "I'll need a helper to pick up the laundry and then take it back for me. What about it? Would you do that? Starting next week, it would mean cycling to Hethel on Saturdays."

"Mum, you know I don't like hanging around airfields," David teased.

"Cheeky boy! That's a yes then?"

"Righto," he said excitedly.

Saturday, after chores, David couldn't wait to tell Roger and Mac the news. He rode in their direction to meet them, feeling the warmth of the late morning sun promising to take some of the chill from the air.

"Guess what?" he said, as they slowed and met. "Starting next Saturday, I have a job. I'll be going to Hethel every week for a laundry run for Mum. It'll take up some time, so I guess I won't get to ride to as many bases anymore."

"Hethel's a good place," Mac said. "It's got B-24 Liberators. Let's see if we can find one today with no one around and climb in."

"Have you gone mental?" David said. "Even if we did

find one, which I doubt, MPs would get us and throw us in jail."

"We wouldn't go to jail," Mac said. "We're just kids."

"Well, the least they would do is throw us off the base and tell our parents. And I'd rather be in jail than face Grandfather," David said.

Ignoring David, Mac asked, "Are you scared, too, Roger?"

"No. But I'd rather look at some B-17 Flying Fortresses today."

"Yeah," David agreed. "Me, too."

Mac looked disappointed. "You're no fun."

They rode to the nearest base at Snetterton, parked their bikes and hung over the fence by the field.

"Thirteen guns. No wonder they call B-17s Flying Fortresses," Roger said.

David added, "Grandfather says a formation of B-17s doesn't need much fighter protection. They can shoot in all directions."

"But look at the holes in that plane!" Mac argued, pointing at flak holes torn in the side of the B-17. "Looks like those guns don't help much against ground fire."

"Daylight bombing seems crazy—the Yanks take a beating," Roger agreed. "They might hit their targets better, but they make an easier target, too."

"I say it's a good plan," David retorted. "How long can the Germans last when they're getting bombed round-the-clock?"

Mac fidgeted impatiently. "O.K., you've seen the B-17s. Let's go to Hethel now. I like the Liberators."

"You just want to find one so you can get into trouble," David said, giving him a friendly shove. But he was glad to head north to Hethel. He liked B-24 Liberators, too.

They had the road to themselves as they pedaled down the lane. Almost no cars traveled because of fuel rationing. After a while, they stopped to eat their sandwiches. David's had Spam in it, the first meat he'd had in a sandwich in months. His mother had waited with others for hours at the grocer's to get it. He enjoyed every bite.

"Since I'll be at Hethel every week," David said, "I'm going to pick my own special plane to keep up with, just like I was part of the ground crew. I'm going to get a notebook and keep track of names and tail numbers of some of the other planes, too. That way, I'll have a record of which ones don't make it back from a mission."

"Great idea," Roger said.

Mac grinned, wiping crumbs from his mouth. "If we're separated sometime, we can report to each other about important stuff at other bases, too."

They mounted their bikes and rode on. As they pulled up to the Hethel fence, David saw a familiar bomber. "I like *Pugnacious Patty*," he said, reading the name printed on the left side of the plane's nose. "She's the one I'm going to adopt."

Roger whistled. "I know why. You like that body in the underwear, huh?"

"What does pugnacious mean, anyway?" Mac asked.

"It means ready to fight," David answered.

"Well, *Fightin' Sam* sounds tougher," Roger said. "I saw that one yesterday. I'll adopt it. I like the word fightin' better than pugnacious, anyway."

"I'll take *Delectable Doris*," Mac said. "Even though I can't spell delectable."

As they walked around the outside of the field, they watched mechanics working on damaged planes.

"They're too busy to notice us," Mac grumbled. "No chance we'll get asked to come over today."

"It's hard to believe they can get those torn-up planes ready to fly again," David said. "But somehow, they do. They'll be working all night."

"I wonder what the men looked like who made it back in those planes," Roger added.

"Or if all of them were alive," Mac said.

David liked being close to the aircraft. It made him feel connected, somehow, to the planes and the crews. He could only read about his own country's planes, since the high fences around the RAF bases kept them at a distance. Watching from afar wasn't nearly as much fun as this.

David hardly noticed the sun beginning to dip in the western sky until Roger said, "It's going to be dark soon. Blast! I hate these short days, Mac. We'd better hurry so we can get home while we can still see."

"Me, too," David said. "I can't be late for milking, or Grandfather will have my hide."

"I'll beat you both," Mac cried, and took off, his short legs pedaling furiously.

As they got to David's turnoff, he called, "See you Monday." His breathless friends waved over their shoulders.

David didn't envy Roger and Mac's ride into Norwich. With the blackout enforced, no lights would help them see. No street signs were anywhere. Even city names were not displayed. The plan was to keep any Germans who parachuted into England from knowing where they were. It was a good idea, David thought, but it made finding the way home in the dark difficult for the Brits as well.

After milking and the evening meal, David gathered with his family in the oak-paneled sitting room to wait for the 9:00 p.m. BBC news. The blackout curtains were drawn, and the fire made the large room cozy, sending flickers of light across the oak-beamed ceiling. It was nice to have everyone home; no one was on volunteer duty tonight.

Nana brought them each a steaming mug with a small portion of hot cocoa. David sat on the sofa with his mother as she mended clothes. Nana joined them. Mary quietly worked on farm accounts, sitting at a small table in the corner in an antique chair that creaked every time she moved. Grandfather leaned back in his sagging brown chair with a newspaper, and Dickens curled up on his lap. Grandfather didn't seem as scary when he was stroking the cat. As David began his first entries in his new aviation notebook, he savored each sip of the rationed cocoa.

The announcer's voice was always the same dull, unemotional monotone. But David liked the war correspondents' reports about the Allies' progress. He liked Winston Churchill's inspiring speeches, too. They made him feel hopeful.

As the announcer talked, David studied the large world map Grandfather had tacked onto the wall. Red pins marked the German advances, blue pins showed the Allied positions. Grandfather moved the pins at the end of each newscast.

There was a 9:30 p.m. broadcast from Germany with the report by Lord Haw Haw, the British traitor who had joined the Nazis. David had never heard it. Boasting of

Germany's power, Haw Haw's radio propaganda was meant to weaken England's morale. Instead, the British found him entertaining. Once, David had asked Grandfather if they could listen. Grandfather had erupted, "That lying traitor's voice will never be heard in this house!" And that was that. David knew better than to try to plead his case further.

Still, David wanted to hear what the boys at school talked and laughed about—Lord Haw Haw's lies about the supposed Nazi victories. Underneath their laughter, though, David could detect some worry about the coming "secret weapon" that Haw Haw said would destroy England and her allies.

As the news ended, David drained the last drop of cocoa from his mug. "Do you think the Nazis really have a secret weapon?" he asked.

"Where did you hear about that?" his mother asked.

David hated to even mention Lord Haw Haw's name in Grandfather's presence.

"They were talking about it at school at lunch," he said.

Grandfather switched off the radio. His mouth formed a hard line. "If there is a secret weapon, we will deal with it," he said firmly. "Probably just more lies from that traitor. Wasted time, listening to that blasted bloke. I'm going to bed. Good night."

David hoped with all his heart the secret weapon *was* just a lie. If not, how would they "deal with it"? The question hung in his mind, unanswered.

CHAPTER 9

Within a few weeks, David, Roger and Mac had notebooks full of information about the Yanks' planes. They recorded different aircraft at various bases: the B-24 Liberators with their wide, double tails; the B-17 Flying Fortresses with their many gun turrets; the red-nosed P-47 Thunderbolt fighters with their red, yellow and blue rudders; and the newer P-51 Mustang fighters, the first long-range pursuit planes.

David had read in the newspaper that the new Mustang fighters, with their Rolls-Royce engines, had made a big difference in the air war. They could carry enough fuel to defend the Liberators all the way to their target. When the formation of American bombers drew German fighter planes up into the sky, the Mustangs could take them on. Grandfather said the bomber pilots called the fighters their "little friends."

David recorded tail numbers, squadron letters and tail fin colors. He liked to check on his favorite planes and write down which ones had what damage and which ones hadn't made it back from a mission. So far, *Pugnacious Patty* had made it with comparatively minor damage. He started making wooden models of the planes he liked.

During the week, he kept track of the planes on "his" Attlebridge airfield when they returned from a mission. He wrote notes to Mac and Roger when a plane didn't return. Keeping his record book and pencil in his coat pocket made it easy to keep records between school and chores.

As the weather warmed in April, he left his coat hanging on the hook by the back door and wore a heavy sweater instead. Each time he checked on Attlebridge planes, he grabbed the book out of the coat pocket, recorded the information and replaced the notebook.

One evening after milking, David came in to find the jacket gone.

"Mum, where's my coat?" he asked, alarmed.

"It was dirty. I took it to the cleaners in Norwich."

"Did you get the notebook out of the pocket?"

"Oh dear, no. I forgot to check the pockets." She looked distressed, then brightened. "I know the young lady at the cleaners. Your name's in the coat. Surely she checked the pockets and would have saved it." Then she added as an afterthought, "If she wasn't too distracted. She was flirting with an American airman when I went in."

"Oh, no!"

"I'll go by tomorrow on my way home from the factory," his mother said apologetically. "I know your record book means a lot to you."

David could hardly sleep that night. All that work. All those records. His latest note to Roger was still in there, too, undelivered. He rode his bike to school the next morning hoping his Mum would have good news waiting for him when he got home.

He'd hardly settled in at his desk when Mr. Hetherington stalked in and stood menacingly over him. "Mr. Freeman, report to my study."

He wanted to ask why, but Mr. Hetherington looked

so ferocious, David just jumped up. As he entered the study, two tough-looking RAF security police glared at him. One was short and stocky, the other tall and lean. The tall one was holding David's coat. The meaty one had his book and the note to Roger.

"Young man, is this your coat?" the tall one asked sternly.

"Yes sir." What on earth!

"Is this your book and your handwriting?" the other inquired in a steely voice.

"Yes sir, that's the book that …"

The tall one interrupted with a look that terrified David. "An American airman was at the laundry when this book and letter were found in the pocket. He believes this to be the work of a spy."

"A spy!" David gasped. He felt his face flush at the accusation. "Sir, I'm not a spy! My father is a Royal Air Force pilot, missing in action. If I could spy, I'd do it against the Germans!" He was humiliated and horrified.

"Careless talk costs lives," the stocky one frowned. "If this information got into the hands of the enemy, it could be dangerous for our men. And obviously, you are careless."

"But sir ..."

"We're confiscating this book," the man said, slapping it against his hand angrily. "You are not to record any information about Allied planes ever again. Understand?"

"Yes sir." David would rather have had a caning than this!

"You're dismissed, Freeman," the headmaster said crisply.

David shoved his hands into his pockets and walked back to class angry and ashamed. A spy! Against the Allies! The very thought made him sick. He hoped his classmates wouldn't find out about that accusation. It would be a stigma to carry around. He vowed never to be careless again. But, he decided, he would not stop checking on his planes. Especially not *Pugnacious Patty*. The Yanks and their planes were his passion. But if Grandfather ever found out he was disobeying the Security Police's orders ...

At lunch, classmates crowded around him to hear what had happened.

"Lost a notebook," he said, dismissively.

Then he whispered the news to Roger and Mac. "But I'm not going to quit taking notes. I'll just write it on the palm of my hand till I can get home to another book. I can erase it with my finger if I get stopped." He took a bite of his sandwich. "And I'll keep my new book hidden in the drawer with my quarter."

"And you thought we'd get in trouble by climbing into a Liberator," Mac said, shaking his head.

David wasn't listening. A terrible thought occurred to him. "What if the MPs went to my house before they came here?" he said, shuddering.

CHAPTER 10

After a week, David decided his secret was safe—unless Mac blurted something out in front of Grandfather.

Today, though, he wouldn't have to worry. Both Mac and Roger were sick and couldn't make their usual Saturday ride with him. David felt a little lonely as he pedaled along the familiar narrow, tree-lined country lane next to Hethel airfield. It seemed oddly quiet.

The chaplain's laundry was neatly folded and tied in the bicycle basket along with the last jar of Nana's elderberry jelly. David was sometimes sorry Nana was so generous with others. With sugar rationing, he didn't know when he'd get a taste of that jelly again. But it was a small price to pay for the joy of riding to Hethel and taking his time.

Grandfather didn't pressure him to hurry back when he was tending to "business," delivering laundry.

When David first met the chaplain, he had expected a solemn older man in a long frock. Instead, he'd found a muscular man in his 20s, doing push-ups on the floor of his Nissen hut. He wore a military uniform with a cross on the collar. David liked his wide smile and funny accent.

Now, David waved to the guard at the main gate. He was allowed in, since the guards knew him from the laundry run. He pedaled to Chaplain's hut and parked his bike beside his.

David tapped on the door.

"Come in!"

David smiled. When Chaplain said "in" it had two syllables—"iyun." He opened the door and grinned at his new friend as he set the laundry on the foot locker at the end of the cot.

Chaplain sat at his small desk, writing a letter. He looked sad.

"Hello, David," he said, with a half-smile. "Good to see you. How've you been?"

"All right, sir. Am I interrupting something?"

"I'm writing a condolence letter to parents whose son was killed," Chaplain said, shaking his head. "It's one of the hardest parts of my job."

"I hope we never get one of those," David said, and his tone sounded angry. "I hope my dad comes home …" His voice trailed.

"Me, too. Since meeting you, I've been praying for your dad. And I have something for you." He picked up a pocket-sized Bible from the desk and handed it to David.

"Thank you, sir." He opened the leather cover and saw, "To David from Chaplain Robert Wilkinson."

Chaplain scooted back in his chair and offered David a seat on an upside-down crate that once held bomb fins.

"I know you're worried and sad, David," he said. "War is terrible. Suffering is terrible. I wish I had some answers. I don't. But I've marked a place for you that has comforted me. I hope it helps."

David opened the Bible to a turned-down page in the book of Joshua. The verse was underlined: "Be strong and courageous," he read aloud. "Do not be afraid or terrified because of them, for the Lord your God goes with you; he will never leave you nor forsake you."

David looked up. "Thanks," he said, wishing it comforted him as much as it did Chaplain. As he slipped the Bible into his sweater pocket, his hand bumped against the jar of jelly.

"Oh!" he said. "I have something for you, too. Elderberry jelly. From Nana, my grandmum." He handed him the jar.

"Hey, that's swell," Chaplain said. "I brought some crackers from the mess hall. Want one with jelly?"

David did, but he said, "No, thanks," even though his mouth was watering. "Nana would want you to have it all."

Chaplain spread a cracker with jelly and popped it into his mouth. "Tell your grandmother I really like it."

"I will. I'd better go, so you can finish your letter."

Chaplain picked up a duffel bag. "Here's next week's laundry. Tell your mother and grandmother I'd like to meet them some time."

"They'd like that, too," David said, taking the bag.

Mounting his bike, he rode out the gate feeling cheerful. He turned down the road and headed to the spot along the edge of the airfield where *Pugnacious Patty* was always parked on the hardstand. The plane wasn't there.

Only one man was. David recognized him as the ground crew chief. He'd seen him often with the whole ground crew, working feverishly on the plane between missions, repairing engines and flak damage, cleaning the plexiglass canopy. He was short, squarely built and very tanned. He always wore a cap, sometimes with the bill turned up. The stocky man shaded his eyes and searched the sky. Was he looking for *Pugnacious Patty?* Feeling bold, David called out to him.

"Hullo, sir!" The man looked over.

"Hi, Kid. Come on over."

David stepped through the hedge and crossed over the field to the hardstand.

"Where's *Pugnacious Patty?*" David asked.

"Not back from her mission yet. What's your name, Son?" he asked.

"David Freeman."

"I'm John, but the guys call me 'Pop.' You can too."

"Thank you, sir. I mean Pop." David instantly liked this man.

"You like planes?" Pop asked.

"Oh, yes sir. My dad's a Royal Air Force pilot—flies, er, flew, a Spitfire. He was shot down." David's voice trailed off. "He's missing."

"I'm sorry. That's a tough deal. I hope he's okay." Pop took a drag off a cigarette, then ground it out underfoot. "You want to meet the crew of the *Pat?*"

"That would be super!" David liked *Pugancious Patty's* nickname, the *Pat.*

"When she comes back, I'll introduce you."

Pop told David about planes and crews and life on the base until the sky filled with the sound of returning Liberators. The rest of the ground crew came out to join them. Still flying in their battle formation, some planes were trailing smoke. They landed first. Then other planes peeled off to land one by one. The four-engine *Pat* landed and taxied to the hardstand. She had heavy flak damage from anti-aircraft ground fire.

The ground crew welcomed the airmen and helped out one man who was limping from an injury. David watched, lost in the excitement.

Then he felt a hand on his shoulder. Pop steered him

to the tall, broad-shouldered pilot who emerged in a heavy flight suit and flak vest. His square-jawed, tanned face was young, but lined with exhaustion. He pulled off his helmet and ran a hand through his blonde hair. He gave Pop a tired smile.

"Tex, this is David," Pop said.

Tex stuck out a big hand. David shook it, noticing it felt tough and calloused. He hoped his own wasn't trembling from excitement. "Hullo, sir."

"Howdy, David." Tex's blue eyes crinkled.

Before they could say more, three MPs drove up in a jeep. David felt a wave of panic. If they were like those RAF officers …

"Get the kid off the field," one said gruffly to Tex.

"Now fellas, I know you're just trying to do your job," Tex drawled. "But I want this kid to stay awhile. I think he's gonna be good luck." He winked at David. "I guess you men have three options," he said, drawing himself up to his full height and stepping toward the military policemen. "One: You can shoot me, which I doubt you want to do. Two: You can confine me to my barracks, which would be great, since I wouldn't have to fly any more missions, or Three: You can get your country tails out of here."

The MPs grumbled and left. David laughed silently.

Tex laid a hand on David's shoulder and said, "Want to see the damage?" He led him around the plane, pointing out the jagged metal around gaping flak holes. "We were lucky to make it back with only a few injuries," he said. "The flak was so thick you could walk on it."

Pop came over. "The crew's going to debriefing now," he explained to David as the crew truck arrived.

"See you," Tex said, as he and his crew climbed into the back of the truck and headed for the Nissen hut more than a mile away.

David waved.

"Want to take a look inside the plane?" Pop asked when they were gone.

"Yes sir!" David said, almost jumping with excitement.

"You'll find some candy in small wax cartons in there. You can have them," Pop said.

David climbed in, feeling like he was in a wonderful

dream. He couldn't believe his luck. Roger and Mac would never believe this. As he walked through the back end of the plane looking for cartons, he was astonished at the huge number of spent brass cartridge cases from the guns. Holes were everywhere, and blood was spattered in places. It seemed odd to be collecting candies where such a life-and-death struggle had taken place.

"Better come on out now," Pop said. "We've got a lot of work to do. And we wouldn't want those MPs coming back."

David jumped down with his pockets bulging.

"Thank you, Pop. That was smashing! I've wanted to see inside a B-24 ever since I first saw them. And the *Pat* is my favorite."

Pop put out his hand and David pumped it hard.

"Come back any time," Pop said. Several members of the ground crew smiled at him as he turned to leave. They were already starting to work on the plane.

"I will," David called as he ran to his bicycle. He was so happy he felt like shouting. Then, as he swung his bike onto the road, reality hit him like a slap. It was late afternoon, and he'd be late for milking. All the way home, he tried to think of ways to appease Grandfather. What if he kept him away from Tex and Pop and the *Pat* as punishment? He'd never pedaled so hard and fast in his life.

CHAPTER 11

Mary was milking when he rushed, breathless, into the barn.

"Where have you been?" she frowned. "I've put in a long day already, and this is your job."

"Sorry," David said, relieved she was alone. "Where is Grandfather?"

"He had to leave early for Home Guard. Lucky for you."

"Lucky for me, if you won't tell."

"I won't. But you owe me a big favor," she said with a wicked smile.

"I'll do anything," David said with relief. "Mary, you won't believe what happened to me today." He washed up in the pan of water and sat down to milk, talking almost as fast as Mac, telling her everything.

"And you know," he said, thoughtfully, "Pop didn't even ask me if I had a sister. He just let me inside the plane to be nice."

Mary laughed.

"Nana and Mum have been talking about asking some of the Americans to tea," Mary said. "Mum wanted to invite a crew and the chaplain. Maybe you could invite your new friends."

"Smashing idea!" David said.

The next morning, a cold, steady rain began and didn't let up. Monday, at school, David told Roger and Mac about Tex and the crew. They immediately began planning to ride with him to Hethel the next weekend. But rains kept them away.

David was secretly glad. He didn't want Mac to monopolize the time with Tex.

"What'll I do about delivering Chaplain's laundry?" David asked his mother the next Saturday. "I don't mind getting soaked, but it'll be hard to keep the laundry dry."

"I can take you to Hethel," Grandfather offered. He was allowed a car and petrol for his war work. He rarely took advantage of it, and David jumped at the offer.

The grounded crews were on base. David introduced his grandfather to Tex and Pop as well as the chaplain. Men were scattered in the quarters, writing letters, playing poker, reading and talking.

After they'd visited a bit, Pop said, "Well, while you boys have fun, I gotta go work in the rain." He grumbled good-naturedly, "Even when you flyboys can have the day off, we can't."

"We'd better leave, too," Grandfather said. He and David walked out with Pop.

"Fine chaps," Grandfather commented on the way home. "We should have them over to the house sometime."

"When?" David asked excitedly.

"We'll let the cooks figure that out. We've got other work to do."

"I'll ask Mum if we can have them the week after Roger's birthday. He'll be 13 next Saturday." David started to ask his grandfather if he could accept Roger's invitation to the birthday dinner and to stay overnight, but he lost his nerve.

All week, the rain kept up. David wore his navy blue

school raincoat each morning as he pedaled to class, but he still arrived cold and wet. Finally, the day of Roger's birthday, the rain let up. David, Mary and Grandfather sat at the kitchen table finishing a late lunch and watching the April sky lighten.

"I'm glad Nana and Mum didn't have to walk in the rain to teach their cookery class in the village," Mary said.

"Sounds like the Yanks are glad the rain has stopped, too," David said, as the roar of bomber engines began at Attlebridge.

"Odd time for them to be leaving, though," Grandfather said, looking at his watch as planes thundered overhead. "Leaving now, they won't be back until dark, and they never fly at night. I wonder what's going on?"

"Could it be the invasion of Europe?" David asked. Everyone had been wondering when they were going to take back those countries Hitler had conquered.

"Too late in the day for that," Grandfather said. Puzzled, they finished their lunch in silence.

"When I take Chaplain's laundry today, I'll ask him what's going on," David said, "and why they're flying so late." Then he forced himself to ask the question he'd been afraid to ask all week. "Grandfather, it's Roger's birthday. His mum's asked me to dinner and said I could stay the night. Could I? I'll work extra hard tomorrow to make it up."

"Who's going to do your part of the milking in the morning?" Grandfather frowned.

David looked at Mary pleadingly. "Mary, if you would, I'll pay you back."

"Then you'd owe me TWO things," Mary said.

David felt his face flush as Grandfather looked his way.

"What else do you owe Mary?" Grandfather demanded, raising an eyebrow.

"Just a bet he lost, Granddad," Mary said, winking at David. "I'll do it this once," she added.

"Thanks, Mary." He took a last bite and said, "I guess I'll make the laundry run now. I'll be back in time to milk before I go to Roger's."

Chaplain's hut was empty when David got to Hethel. He dropped the laundry off, picked up the new batch, then rode to the *Pat's* hardstand. She was gone, too. He pedaled back home, puzzled, with a strange quivery feeling in his stomach. What was going on?

"So happy you could come, David," Roger's mother said, as she opened the door to let him in.

"I'm glad the rain's stopped. Mmmm. Smells good in here."

"We'll eat in a few minutes," she smiled. "Roger's upstairs waiting for you."

David hurried up the narrow stairs. Roger was in his room painting a model airplane.

"Hullo. Happy Birthday!" David said. "Great plane. Where'd you get silver paint? I've been trying to find some for my model of the *Pat* that I'm making for Tex."

"My parents got it for my birthday. I'll lend you some. Did Tex fly today? I saw all the planes going over after lunch. Started to ride over to your house, but decided not to. Figured there wouldn't be much to see at the airfields."

"I went out to Hethel. The *Pat* was gone," David said. "It's strange. Why do you think they left so late?"

"I don't know, but it couldn't have been a regular mission. I wonder when they'll be back? If it's after dark, I guess the airfields can't be blacked out; they'll have to turn on their lights to guide them in."

"Maybe we can watch them come over," David said.

"Boys, time for supper," Roger's mother called.

They sat down to the steaming meal. David was hungry; it seemed the faster he grew, the less the rationed food allowance filled him. He always cleaned his plate and wished for more. He was excited that tonight they'd finish with birthday cake. As they lingered at the table, David enjoyed the easy laughter in Roger's family. It reminded him of how his family used to laugh when his dad was home.

David thought Roger was lucky to have his dad. Because his eyesight was bad, his father hadn't gone to war. But, Roger seemed a little embarrassed that his dad had to do the war work of older, less able-bodied men.

After cake, Roger's father left for Home Guard duty, and the boys helped with the dishes. When they heard the returning formation's deep rumble, they exchanged excited glances.

"Mum, can we go look at them?" Roger asked.

"What can you see in the dark?"

"They'll turn on their landing lights. I've never seen Liberators at night. Please!" he pleaded.

"Silly boy. Go on then!" She smiled.

David and Roger scrambled out the door.

"We're just in time. They're putting their lights on," Roger said, pointing at the large formation.

Suddenly, gunfire erupted. David squatted down instinctively, his eyes still on the sky. A Liberator burst into flames.

"Germans!" David yelled. "Must have hidden in the formation." Panic gripped him.

Suddenly everyone was shooting at everyone else, and Roger's mother rushed out to pull the boys inside. David watched from the doorway, unbelieving, as a B-24, flaming from nose to tail, flew low along the road only yards away. It was so close, he felt the heat.

"It's going to crash!" Roger cried.

"Oh, God help them," his mother moaned.

David winced at the sound of the explosion. As all of them rushed out of the house and ran down the road toward the flames, David's legs could hardly propel him forward. He felt like a weakling. Pieces of aircraft lay burning all around. It had missed the houses, but the scene was horrible.

"Stand back," Roger's mother said, her voice hoarse with grief as the main part of the plane was consumed by fuel-fed flames. "It's too late. We can't do anything."

Even at a distance, the heat was intense. David's mouth was dry. Who had been in that plane? It was impossible to read tail numbers or a name. He turned his face away from the awful sight. What if it was Tex and his crew? What Yanks had lost their lives only minutes from safety? He kicked dirt over a small patch of burning grass and blinked back tears.

What were those last dreadful moments like for those men? David couldn't imagine. He didn't want to. It stirred up too many doubts about himself.

He stuffed his hands into his pockets, trying to stop the uncontrollable shaking. If he had the shakes now, it flashed through his mind, how would he react as a pilot in an emergency? He clenched his fists angrily, hoping the RAF night fighters could chase and shoot down those sneaky murderers. If his dad were here, he would have gone after them. David wished he were more like his fearless dad.

He remembered Grandfather's advice that day in the barn when they were having words about David's exams: "Set your mind to it."

All right, David decided, he would set his mind to it. Whatever the dangers, whatever it took, he would force himself to become a brave fighter pilot. He never wanted to say, "We can't do anything."

Ambulance and fire sirens screamed closer. Neighbors gathered, cursing the enemy and putting out small fires with sandbags.

"I hope the RAF gets them," David said to Roger as they dragged back to Roger's house.

David hardly slept that night. He prayed a long time, hoping Chaplain's favorite verse was true, and that God had been with those men. But it was all so hard to understand. Even Chaplain had said he couldn't explain suffering, and that he just clung to the only hope he had: his faith that this life wasn't all there is. David would cling to that, too.

"Please give me courage," he whispered into the darkness. "Help me."

As soon as it was light enough to ride, David pedaled home from Roger's, feeling terribly tired, noticing patches of melted aluminum from the plane on the road surface. He turned before he reached the crash scene. Heartsick, he couldn't stand to look at it again. He couldn't bear to think it might be Tex and his crew.

CHAPTER 13

"**D**avid!" His mother hugged him hard. Nana and Mary looked worried.

"We heard what happened at Norwich. Was it near you? Did you see it?"

"It was almost on Roger's doorstep," he nodded. "Mum, I've got to know if it was Tex and his crew."

"Your grandfather went to check with the chaplain. He should be back any time," Nana told him.

"Tell us what you saw," his mother said, steering him to the sofa. She sat down beside him. Nana brought him a cup of tea. He began to shake again as he told them all he knew. The back door opened and Grandfather walked in. They looked at him expectantly.

"It wasn't your crew, David. They are all right, but very shaken," he said.

David breathed a sigh of relief as Grandfather continued, "Chaplain took me with him to the barracks. He said he'd gone last night to comfort the crews. They were angry and shocked and very sad, cursing those Germans and even themselves for letting something like that happen. Their mission had been a tough one, and they were so relieved to be almost home. They're all feeling somehow to blame for their friends' deaths."

"Poor lads!" Nana said. "I hate this war."

David's mother sighed, shaking her head.

"Mum, Nana, we could cheer them up a bit," David suggested. "Could we invite Tex's crew here next weekend? We've been talking about having them to dinner."

"But we were trying to save up some of our rations," Mary said. "We haven't gathered enough yet. We couldn't have them all."

"Nonsense," Nana told her. "In my cookery classes I teach how to stretch what you have. We'll make do. David, ride over as soon as you can and ask them to come Saturday, if they're not flying. You can ask your friend Pop and the chaplain if they'd like to come too."

"Grandfather, we could go hunting and bring in some meat," David suggested.

His grandfather smiled slightly, the first smile David had seen in a long time. "We could do that," he said. "It would feel good to do something for the lads. Maybe someone is doing something for our boy, too," he added, giving Nana's arm a quick squeeze.

"Think we could be forgiven for cheating and keeping some of our cream to make butter?" Nana asked. "It would make everything taste so much better."

"I'll bet the government wouldn't send us to jail for feeding the Yanks," Grandfather said. "Where would we be without them? Maybe the cows will cooperate and give us a little extra next weekend."

The week dragged by, even though the family was busy preparing for the party. Saturday evening finally arrived, and a big American supply truck with a white star on its door pulled up. Young men poured out the back.

David watched out the window as Tex and Pop together led 10 men to the door. Nana and Grandfather opened it.

"Howdy, I'm Tex. You're swell to have us," Tex said as he handed Nana a tin of fruit and some chocolate.

She looked embarrassed. "Oh, please, no gifts!"

"It's nothing," Tex said. "We're just so glad to get away from the barracks and into a real home again." He looked David's way. "Hi, hoss! Haven't seen you in awhile!" He slapped David on the shoulder. Then his eyes moved to Mary, and David saw them sparkle. His smile grew broader.

"I'm Tex," he said, taking off his pilot's cap and keeping his eyes on her.

"I'm Mary," she said, flushing a little and then looking away from his admiring gaze.

Tex turned, sweeping his arm across the crowd of nine young men and said, "And these are my crew. I'll let them introduce themselves." He put his hand on Pop's shoulder. "But this is Pop, who heads up the ground crew, and this is Chaplain Bob, who only looks sharp because you wash and iron for him." He grinned. The others laughed.

As they served their plates, Tex admired David's model airplanes that he'd put in the center of the table.

Tex asked about the Blitz and what it was like to be bombed, and Mary told him about it shyly as he took a seat next to her. Mike, Tex's co-pilot, sat on the other side of her. David sat cross-legged on the floor near them, adding his comments to Mary's. But it seemed the men only glanced his way briefly. Mary was definitely the center of attention.

"This is delicious, ladies," Tex said, taking a big bite. "Sure beats the mess hall stew."

"I've been missin' my Mom's cookin'," said one. "This homemade bread reminds me of hers."

"You don't chicken-fry steak, do you?" another joked.

Tex turned to Mary. "We're sure glad to be in a home again. My folks will appreciate your hospitality to us. I can't wait to tell them about your thatched roof, too. Never saw anything like it, except in picture books."

"Where is your family?" Mary asked.

"On a ranch in West Texas. I grew up there. Spent my life herding cattle horseback, and farming wheat. Back home, they'd give a million bucks for some of the rain you have here."

"I just wish I didn't have to fly in it," Mike said to

Mary. "When our planes are forming up in the mornings, the sky is like a thick soup of fog and rain."

"And collisions happen sometimes, when you can't see," Tex said regretfully, "in spite of careful spacing."

"How perfectly awful," Mary said.

David thought Mike and Tex were battling for Mary's attention. In fact, it seemed everyone directed their comments to Mary. No one looked his way at all.

He glanced around at his family. Grandfather's face looked happier than he'd seen it in a long time. Mum and Nana smiled contentedly. But Mary looked happiest.

As the young men told about their families back home, their lives before the war, their sweethearts left behind, David realized what they'd given up to fight Hitler. Pop, the only married one, said the others had allowed him to name the *Pat* after his wife Patty. He showed them a picture of her. She looked nothing like the girl on the front of the plane.

"I only got to name the plane. The others chose the nose art," Pop said, almost apologetically. "I hope Patty never sees it."

"She might not like it that I added Pugnacious to her

name, either," Tex smiled.

As David looked around at his new friends, he wondered sadly if they'd all be able to get back home to their families safely. He knew the odds were against it.

He heard the arrival of the Liberty Run truck, which nightly picked up off-duty airmen from the cinema and pubs in Norwich. Tex's crew reluctantly stood to leave.

"Thanks a million," Tex said. "This has been a great evening." The others echoed their thanks. Tex slapped David on the back.

"Next time you ride out and we're not flying, bring those two buddies you've been talking about. We'll get you all into the mess hall for some ice cream."

"We'll be there." David grinned. He was glad Tex had at last paid some attention to him.

Nana closed the door, and they all began gathering dishes to wash. Grandfather whistled, Nana hummed and Mary seemed lost in thought. David was happy, yet a little annoyed at Mary for attracting all the attention. But, he thought, if he was smart, he could use it to his own advantage.

"Did you like Tex?" he asked.

"Yes," she said dreamily. "He's very nice."

"You wouldn't have met him if I hadn't met him first," he said.

"Mmm hmm," she said absently.

"So I think tonight should pay back both the favors I owe you."

She seemed to come alive. "Cheeky devil!" she laughed. "Maybe I didn't like him very much."

"What do you say? If I dry all the dishes, are we even?"

She flipped dishwater at him with her fingers. "Yes, but I'm sure it won't be for long. You and those airplanes …!"

"Bother," he said, "You'll probably start owing *me.*"

But he knew that Mary was probably right—he'd need more favors. He intended to spend as much time as possible at the airfield while he could. Once the school summer holiday arrived, farm chores increased. He'd have almost no time off. And Grandfather got even crankier when there was more work to be done.

CHAPTER 14

Even with a little free time, David didn't get to see Tex much. But he spent hours standing with Pop and his friends searching the sky for the *Pat*. Many times, the planes flew home in formation. Whenever he saw a blank spot in a returning formation, his stomach tightened. Was that spot where the *Pat* should be? Straining to see the scantily clad girl painted on the plane's front, or the familiar tail letters of D+, he felt huge relief when he finally saw his B-24 land and taxi toward them.

David knew when a flare was fired from a crippled plane, it signaled trouble or that severely wounded were on board. Fire trucks and ambulances rushed out to greet those planes. Even without a flare shot from the *Pat*, however, David couldn't fully relax until Tex's crew, sometimes bloodied, stepped out. He wanted to hug Tex in happiness each time he saw his tired, lanky friend. He looked forward to their repeated ritual—Tex leading him around the aircraft, hand on his shoulder, showing him the damage.

"I think you're good luck," Tex said one day. "We've had a lot of near misses. Like today." He shook his head sadly and continued, "The '24 right in front of us took a direct hit. Blew up!" Tex cleared his throat as if sorrow had suddenly choked him.

David didn't know about luck, but he knew that before every mission, Tex and many of the others went to chapel with the chaplain. Sometimes he took David, too. And once, Chaplain had broken the rules and flown with them on a mission, praying the whole way. Whatever was keeping Tex safe, David hoped it kept on working. He couldn't lose both Tex and his dad.

When Tex and the crew were resting, David, Roger and Mac spent time with Pop. They watched him and the ground crews work. Pop taught them about the cockpit instruments and controls and the positions each airman manned in the aircraft.

David was fascinated with the rear turret, a plexiglass bubble that held two machine guns and was at the tail of the plane. One man sat in the tail turret, which could be moved up, down and all around. David wondered what it would be like to be there alone, like a sitting duck, firing as German fighters attacked.

Tex had told David the crew wore electrically-heated suits and oxygen masks, because as they flew at 20,000–30,000 feet, the temperature dipped to more than 20 degrees below zero. And, if an oxygen mask froze up, or a suit malfunctioned, the man in it would die. The crew looked after one another. David wondered how the lonely ball turret gunner felt with no partner to check on him. Being a pilot would be much better, he thought.

David never knew where the crew was headed when they took off on a mission. That sort of information was secret. Tex had told him even the crews weren't fully informed until their pre-mission briefings, the morning of takeoff. At that time, officers in the briefing room uncovered a large map revealing the day's target and route, then gave crews the plans.

David learned about missions on the news when they were completed. He'd heard that Allied planes had been bombing the launching sites for Germany's "secret weapon," V-Weapons, flying bombs that didn't need airplanes or pilots. The enemy's V-Weapons research base had been bombed, too. David hoped the Allies could wipe out those flying bombs before they were ever launched toward England.

Tex told David that Pop and the ground crew's work, servicing and repairing the *Pat,* was crucial. David often had watched Pop check out the serviced engines by doing a "ground run," running up the engines as the plane sat still with brakes locked and wheels chocked with blocks.

One day, when David was alone at the field, Pop said, "Do you want to sit in the cockpit with me for the ground run? You can press the starter switches and operate the throttles."

Did he want to! David had never had so much fun. Feeling the power under his hand as he revved up the engines made his heart leap. The more he was in and around airplanes, the more he knew that someday, he had to fly. What he lacked in courage, he'd make up for in skill.

"Duck if you see an MP's jeep," Pop said. "Wouldn't want to get us in trouble."

David wasn't so worried about MPs. If they came around, at least he had Tex and Pop to defend him. But he did worry about Grandfather. If Grandfather decided David was neglecting school and the farm, he'd stop letting him come. And he'd probably give Mary the laundry run. So David had been working harder than ever. His marks on exams had improved somewhat, too. But Grandfather never praised him. David wished his grandfather were more like his dad—smiling and encouraging.

Pop, however, seemed to have confidence in him. "I'll trust you boys in the cockpit if you won't touch the controls," he told them one day. Pop let David and his friends put on headsets and pretend to fly. Trying to sound official, they'd used the correct radio procedure, and David made an effort to drawl like Tex. Pop roared with laughter.

David enjoyed the Yanks' easy laughter. They brought it into his house when they came to visit. But there were also times when the men came quietly, saying little, when their friends hadn't returned from a mission. On occasion, Tex came alone, settling down on the sofa by

Mary, his long legs stretched out comfortably. The family talked with him for awhile, and then it seemed Nana and Mum always invented a way to draw David and Grandfather out of the room.

Once, David had overheard Tex confide to Mary that he was having trouble sleeping at night. "I can't shut my mind off, thinking what the next day's mission might bring," he said. "And, even though it might seem strange, the thought of being killed isn't as bad as the fear that I might panic or be a coward and fail my squadron mates." Tex had paused and looked down at his boots. "I've never confessed that to anyone before."

As Mary comforted Tex with words so low David couldn't hear them, David had felt great comfort himself. Tex doubted his own bravery. Maybe, David thought, courage was not fearlessness. It was doing the job in spite of fear.

David was glad Tex had Mary. He was glad all the men seemed to take comfort being in a home. But he felt a terrible heaviness knowing that any evening, one or more of the crew might be permanently missing. He couldn't imagine life if Tex didn't return.

CHAPTER 15

Something was going on, David was sure. British Army crews were on the move.

"Those tanks are huge!" David exclaimed one Saturday, as he, Roger and Mac pulled their bicycles to a stop along the road. Village children joined the crowds gathering. They all stared in awe as the monstrous, camouflaged machines rumbled past. David had never seen tanks before.

"Self-propelled guns!" Mac said, pointing, as the heavy guns rolled past with their crews.

"I heard they're parked all around Eaton Park, too," Roger said. "Squadrons of them. And the Royal Scottish Artillery's heavy field guns."

That night, Grandfather explained, "They must be preparing for the invasion of Europe, waiting for orders to move down to the South Coast. The invasion must be close!"

"Do the Germans know we're coming?" David asked.

"Yes, they know we must invade if we intend to free the occupied countries. But they don't know where we will land. Or when. Hitler has taken over so much territory that he is spread thin trying to defend it all. He's trying to fortify the whole coast so we can't land. Our invasion will be a huge, dangerous undertaking, and it's important that Hitler not figure out where we'll come ashore or when."

David wondered what that day would be like.

In the pre-dawn darkness on June 6, 1944, he found out. He woke to the most awesome roar of airplanes he had heard yet. Even the Blitz couldn't equal it. Nonstop, wave after wave of planes vibrated the house.

"Mum, Mary, hear that?" he said, knowing they, too, would be awake now.

"The Allies must be invading the continent!" his mother said. "At last! The day we've been waiting for!" They dressed quickly and rushed outdoors.

"There must be thousands and thousands of them,"

Mary said. "God protect them!"

"Especially Tex and his crew," David whispered, staring into the sky.

At breakfast, Grandfather confirmed it. "No doubt about it. The invasion has begun. It will be tough. God help us if Hitler's ready!"

Just after 9:30 a.m., they heard the news on the radio. "This is the BBC Home Service," the announcer in London began. "Early this morning the Allies began the assault on the northwestern face of Hitler's European fortress.... Under the command of General Eisenhower, Allied naval forces, supported by strong air forces, began landing Allied armies on the northern coast of France ..."

David wanted to cheer, but the mood in the kitchen was somber. The undertaking would cost thousands of lives. And if it weren't successful ... David couldn't think about it. It *had* to succeed. As he worked through the morning, his stomach was in knots wondering if Tex and his crew had made it, and if the landing was successful. All afternoon, he saw wave after wave of planes returning. He wished he could be at the airfield.

When Saturday finally arrived, David could hardly wait for Roger and Mac to get to his house so they could bike to Hethel. He thought he would have heard from Chaplain if Tex hadn't made it back from the invasion they now knew as D-Day. But he couldn't be sure. All he knew was the number of Allied casualties, especially the ground troops, had been shocking.

At last Roger and Mac rode up, and David joined them, pedaling eagerly toward Hethel. As they pulled up to the *Pat's* hardstand, David was disappointed. The plane was gone.

"Tex is fine," Pop told them. "Out on another mission. The crew may be flying several a day now." Looking at their fallen faces, he added, "Would it cheer you up to go to the mess hall with me today?"

"Yes, sir!" they cried in unison. While they wolfed down fried chicken followed by ice cream, David and Roger listened as the Yanks told them about the masses of ships in the English Channel and the long route they had to take to form up before heading for Normandy's beaches on D-Day.

David noticed Mac was too busy talking to listen. He

chattered to Pop about the 22,000 pounds of bombs a British Lancaster could carry. "That's three times as many as a B-24," he said. "And I read that a Lancaster uses only about half the distance to take off that a B-24 needs," he added proudly. "Amazing," Pop smiled. He seemed to understand Mac's pride in the RAF. And if he didn't believe everything Mac said, he didn't show it.

After lunch, with his stomach feeling full for the first time in ages, David said, "Thank you, Pop! We'll come later and see if the *Pat's* back. I guess I'd better deliver Chaplain's laundry now."

With Roger and Mac echoing thanks, the three boys rode off again. Chaplain wasn't in, but David left the bundle and picked up the new batch.

"Chaplain must be visiting at the hospital," David said.

"We could ride over and watch what's going on from the road," Roger suggested. It was a short distance to the U.S. Army Hospital. They looked on as ambulances brought in the wounded they'd picked up from hospital trains at the Wymondham Railway Station.

"There are so many of them," Roger whispered as stretcher after stretcher went inside.

"I hope there's never another day as terrible as the D-Day invasion," David said.

"And I hope Tex and his crew make it back today," Mac added.

"Let's go check one more time," David said, turning his bike around. But he knew the sky was too quiet for planes to be anywhere near.

With a glance at the empty hardstand, David sighed, "I guess I'd better get home. I've still got chores to do." He'd wanted so much to see Tex. It felt as if he were leaving part of his heart at the hardstand.

CHAPTER 16

Weeks later, David still hadn't seen Tex. As he put Chaplain's folded laundry and empty duffel bag in his bicycle basket, he hoped his luck would change today, and Tex would be at the airfield.

He waited for Roger and Mac, thinking about recent newscasts. The Allies were making progress, but the Germans had retaliated by launching their "secret weapon," the pilotless, jet-propelled V-1 bombs. Hundreds of them were being fired toward big cities in England. They flew until the engine stopped, then fell out of the sky and exploded. Luckily, they often went astray, but they destroyed whatever they hit. More than once, sirens had whined their alarm as a rattly V-1 flew over Norwich.

"As long as you can hear the Doodlebug's noisy rattle, you are safe," Grandfather had told him, using the V-1's nickname. "But, when things get suddenly quiet, take cover!"

At last, David saw Mac cycling toward him alone. "Hi. Where's Roger?" David asked.

"His Mum and Dad both have the flu. He had to stay and help."

David was sorry and very disappointed. And now, he thought miserably, he was stuck alone with jabbering Mac. "He's only 10, and he's curious," Roger had said to explain his young cousin. But to David, Mac's rapid-fire questions were like a machine gun that never ran out of ammunition.

"Let's hurry, then," David said, now hoping to pedal fast enough to keep Mac too breathless to talk. It didn't work.

"Think the *Pat's* flying again today?" Mac asked. "Maybe they froze some oranges in the bomb bay for us on the test flight like they did last time. Or maybe the *Pat's* not flying and we can see Tex. Do you think Pop will let us in the cockpit like before? I'd like to be the pilot. I won't touch any switches or anything." Mac talked on and on, and David stopped listening. Soon he heard something else. Sirens.

"And do you think ...," Mac was continuing.

"Shhhh. Listen!" David interrupted. The hair on his neck prickled. He heard the distinct noisy clatter of a Doodlebug. As it drew near, David looked into the sky's glare, trying to see it.

"It's getting close!" David could feel his heart racing. He looked around. A two-story farm cottage was nearby, but no ditch. They could lie flat on the ground. Suddenly, an eerie silence fell over the countryside.

"Get down!" David cried. They jumped off their bikes, and fell to the ground, arms covering their heads. The explosion was ear-splittingly close.

David sat up. He looked across the road. Through heavy smoke, he saw flames shooting up from the back of the farmhouse.

"Look!" he cried. "Someone might be in there!"

He jumped on his bike and raced across the lane and up into the yard. Mac stood back, frozen, watching.

"Hurry!" David called.

Mac didn't move.

David ran toward the burning house. He heard a cry for help. Heart pounding, his mind whirling, he wondered where the cry had come from. What should he do?

CHAPTER 17

Smoke poured from shattered windows. As David reached the porch, an elderly woman stumbled out, holding her bleeding head, coughing.

"My husband!" she cried between gasps. "He's upstairs. He's blind. Help him!"

Some sort of wild energy propelled David through the door. Intense heat hit him like a wall. The smoke was thick. He could hear the loud crackling of fire. He didn't have much time. He had to get up those stairs. He dropped low where the air was more breathable, and half crawled, half ran up the stairs.

"Sir!" he cried. "Where are you?"

"Here," called a voice from the dense fog of smoke.

The man was only a few feet from the top of the steps. David grabbed the thin form and half carried him.

"Careful! Stairs!" he gasped. His stinging eyes watered so much he could hardly see.

"My wife!" the man wheezed.

"Safe," David said. He pulled his shirt up to cover his nose. His lungs hurt. He and the old man coughed and stumbled down the steps together and out the door. With his arm around the man's waist, David hurried him off the porch, away from the smoke. As David gulped in the fresh air, the man almost collapsed.

"Gotta ... get ... farther ... away ...," David coughed. With a firm grip around the man, he pulled him toward the far edge of the yard. Mac ran up to help. The old woman held out her arms to her husband, and held him as he sank down on the grass beside her.

A neighbor ran down the lane toward them. David sat down hard, coughing, his eyes burning. He looked back at the house, now completely engulfed in flames.

"Thank you, thank you," the woman said, tears streaking her smudged face." You're a brave lad. Thank God you were here!"

"Aye! Thank you, laddy," the man whispered hoarsely.

"Help is on the way," the neighbor said, running up. "Do you need help, too, son?"

Fire engine and ambulance sirens sounded.

"I'm all right," David croaked. He wanted to go home. When he stood, he felt light-headed.

Mac ran for his bicycle and brought it to him.

"What's your name?" the woman called as David shakily mounted his bike.

"David Freeman." His voice was faint.

"God bless you, David Freeman."

Mac rode alongside David a long way without talking. David was grateful for the silence and the fresh breeze in his face. Finally, in a voice choked with emotion, Mac said, "I'm sorry that I didn't help. I couldn't do it."

"I was scared, too," David admitted. He didn't know how he'd managed to run in, almost without thinking. Something stronger than himself, braver than he felt, had taken over. Fear had been pushed aside by the need for action—doing what had to be done. Now that it was over, he felt shaky. But back there he'd just done it. Was that how it worked with his dad and Tex, too?

As he walked through the door of his grandfather's house, David felt a crushing fatigue. Nana's mouth dropped open when she saw him.

"Dear God! What happened?" she cried, rushing toward him.

"A Doodlebug. Hit a house. It was burning. I pulled a man out." He slumped into a chair. He was glad his mother wasn't home. Tears weren't far away.

Grandfather came in and listened as David told the story between coughing fits. Nana brought him a wet cloth to wipe his eyes and face. She sat facing him, patting his knee, wide-eyed with worry as he tried to talk. When he finished, he glanced up at his grandfather, still standing above him. He was surprised to see the tough look had softened.

Grandfather put a hand on David's shoulder and said, "I'm glad you're all right, lad. You did a fine thing, risking your life for someone you didn't even know. I'm proud of you, son. Your dad would be, too." He gave his shoulder a squeeze. "You became a man today."

David couldn't speak. Grandfather was proud of him. He'd said he was a man. David sat for a while, waiting for the light-headedness to pass, rubbing the cool cloth over his eyes. He wasn't sure if a man would shake like this, but he did like this new feeling of confidence. He'd been scared, but he'd done something he thought he couldn't do. Maybe that's what it was all about. You just did it.

Then he remembered Tex, and the chaplain's laundry still tied in his basket. "I wish I weren't so tired," he said sadly. "I wanted to go to the airfield."

"I'll take you," Grandfather offered. "Today the work can wait a bit."

As Grandfather pulled the car to a stop on the lane near the *Pat's* hardstand, David saw Pop, Chaplain, and the ground crew waiting for the *Pat* in their usual place. David handed Chaplain the laundry packet and empty duffel bag.

"Not much flak was expected on their mission today," Pop told them. "Supposedly an easy target—a milk run."

David hoped it was. He hoped he could see Tex this time.

David knew from his records that Tex had flown 22

missions as of D-Day. At 35 missions, his tour of duty would be over, and he and the crew could return to the States. With the frequent missions he'd been flying lately, Tex would be finished before long. David had heard him confide once to Mary that the closer a crew got to their final mission, the more nervous they became. Many had lost their lives on a final flight.

David hoped the *Pat* would get back soon, so he could take the "good luck" walk with Tex around the plane again. But it was looking doubtful. It was late afternoon, and David knew Grandfather wouldn't hear of the cows having to wait to be milked. He stole a glance at Grandfather. His face was unreadable.

Just then, he heard the distant drone of engines. As the planes approached, flares shot from several of them, and smoke trailed those planes. David saw the dreaded empty hole in the formation. The mission hadn't been just a milk run. Someone hadn't made it back. He prayed as planes landed. He kept watching for the *Pat*. But she never came.

CHAPTER 18

Cursing, Pop jogged over to talk to another crew whose plane had landed nearby. He came back, shaking his head, jaw clenched.

"They saw the *Pat* take a hit right below the cockpit," he reported. "They were able to release their bombs after they were hit, so that's a good sign. But they had to drop out of formation. Maybe they'll show up in a little while." He took off his cap and rubbed his head.

David waited, pacing back and forth between Pop and Grandfather, cracking his knuckles. He knew that when a plane dropped out of formation it was a sitting duck for enemy fighter planes.

"David, I'm sorry. It's time to go. The cows can't wait any longer," Grandfather said.

"But, Grandfather! I can't leave!"

Grandfather gave him a stern glance.

Pop laid a hand on David's shoulder. "Tex is a great pilot. So is Mike. If the *Pat's* able to fly at all, they'll get her home. Go on. Don't worry."

David didn't think Pop looked as sure as he sounded. And he'd seen Chaplain bow his head in prayer several times. David's worry-knot formed again in his stomach.

"Don't tell Mary," Grandfather ordered as they drove home. "No need to frighten her when we don't know anything."

Mary couldn't be any more frightened than I am, David wanted to say, willing his stomach to stop quivering.

After milking, the hours crawled by. David couldn't concentrate on anything, not even his own story about the fire, which Mary and his mother encouraged him to tell. Exhausted, he went to bed early. Yet he couldn't sleep. He kept thinking about German fighter pilots who watched for lone, crippled bombers to attack. Had Tex's plane, unprotected by their formation and unescorted by their own fighters, been shot down on the way home? Were they forced to ditch or bail out? Was Tex badly wounded if sharp flak fragments had torn through his plane's side? Face hot, his body tense, David tossed about, sick with worry.

He jerked when Grandfather shook his shoulder at 4:30 a.m. He dragged out of bed, dreading the long day at school. How could he concentrate? With final exams right around the corner, he *had* to pay attention.

When he got to school, he was mobbed by his friends. Mac had told everyone about the house fire, and they all wanted to talk about it. David wished he could enjoy his temporary status as hero. But it seemed hollow. He just wished he could do something heroic for Tex.

That night at supper, David thought Mary seemed especially happy. She still didn't know. She talked about the monthly dances at the base, the Glenn Miller band that played, and the loads of girls brought in from Norwich on base trucks. "But Tex only dances with me," she smiled.

"Let me show you what Tex taught me at the dance," she said after dinner.

She pulled David up from his chair. "It's called the jitterbug. It's fun." She showed him the steps, then began pushing and pulling him, spinning. David stumbled over his own feet, uninterested.

"Pay attention. You'll have a girlfriend one day," Mary teased. "Now watch again."

He let go of her hand and sat back down.

"What's wrong with you?" Her smile faded.

"Nothing." He didn't look at her.

"You haven't been yourself since yesterday. Something about the fire?" He could feel her intense gaze. "David?"

Just then he heard a truck. David rushed to the door. Perhaps it was someone with news of Tex! When he saw Chaplain get out of the truck, his heart skipped a beat.

Mary walked over, too. "It's Chaplain! Why is he here? What's going on?"

"He might have some bad news," David warned her, cracking his knuckles nervously. "Brace yourself."

"Hello, David, Mary. Good news," Chaplain beamed. "Tex and his crew are safe. We heard late last night they'd made a forced landing at another base. A miracle that they got their plane that far. Flak hit the oil line. The *Pat's* staying for repairs. But I knew you'd want to hear."

A huge wave of relief swept over David. He grinned.

"Tex didn't come back last night?" Mary asked,

startled. "And you didn't tell me?" She glared at David.

Grandfather joined them. "My idea," he admitted, adding, "Come in, Chaplain."

"Can't tonight. I'm riding the Liberty Truck into Norwich with some of the guys to catch a movie. But I brought the laundry, since I forgot to give it to you yesterday." He handed Grandfather the bag.

"Sorry! We were all a bit distracted," Grandfather smiled, taking the bag. "Thank you for the good report."

As Grandfather shut the door, David turned to Mary with a grin. "O.K. Let's see that jitterbug thing again. I feel like dancing." Yet even as he spun his happy sister, it was hard not to think that Tex's "good luck" could run out any day.

CHAPTER 19

Summer had come. David couldn't put away his school uniform fast enough—the shirt, cap, grey trousers and navy blue blazer with the school badge. He wondered if next fall they would still fit him. Buying the school uniform and his Scout uniform had used up nearly all of his dwindling clothing coupons. He hoped that Nana, whom he teasingly called Mrs. Sew and Sew, could make his uniforms "grow" with him.

As the weather grew hot, he worked hard all week, living for Saturdays when he rode out to Hethel. During the week, as he drove the combine harvester cutting wheat, he watched the planes at *his* airfield. The planes were nearby as he harvested, because every available acre had been planted, even strips beside the runways.

"Get your eyes on your work! Your rows are wavy!"

Grandfather complained.

Having "double summertime," the time change that gave them light until 11:00 p.m., made the days long. David knew that the time change helped factory production as well as drivers, who weren't allowed to put on their lights at dark. But to David, the main thing was the chance to get his work done and still have a bit of daylight for watching planes.

Tex, his crew, and occasionally a Yank whom Nana met at the Red Cross came to the house, often bringing gifts of food and treats. Although Nana protested, it helped stretch their scanty food supply. And David was always happy to see more to eat!

Tex and Mary spent more and more time together. Tex brought her and David copies of the *Yank* and *Stars and Stripes,* their one-page newspapers. David liked the comic strips about Dick Tracy and Terry and the Pirates.

Tex taught them American songs, too, like *Home on the Range.* And he told them, "The Germans play that song on their propaganda station, trying to make us homesick, and then they say, 'You'll never see America again.' That's true for way too many of us. But we're going to win this war, and we are going to go home again."

David knew Tex was getting close to going home. Just three more missions! When Tex left, David knew he would miss him terribly. And he could tell Mary would, too.

The night before Tex's last mission, he came to the house riding Chaplain's bicycle. "Needed a little good luck," he said, ruffling David's hair. Tex looked tired and anxious. "You've helped a lot of us keep our sanity by opening up your home to us," he said to the family. "I wanted to thank you. If we make it back."

"WHEN you make it back," David corrected him.

"When we make it back, I may get shipped out before I can say goodbye. So I wanted to …"

Nana interrupted his speech by hugging him. "We'll be praying for you," she said. "And we're the ones who want to thank you." She looked a little misty-eyed. "Mary, why don't you take Tex out on the porch, and I'll bring you tea in a bit."

As David started to follow them, Nana gently pulled him back. "Let them be, pet."

"But …!"

"How about a game of cards?" his mother offered.

"Never mind. I need to put the finishing touches on my model of the *Pat*. It's for Tex. His going-away present," he said.

Later, as Mary walked Tex to the door, David handed him the carved plane.

"This is swell!" Tex said, admiring it. "Thanks, David! I'll keep this." He ruffled David's hair one last time.

As Tex rode away, fear and sadness gripped David. His throat tightened. One last mission. Just one more. Would Tex and the crew's "luck" hold? David turned and saw his anxiety reflected on the family's faces.

The next afternoon, when it was about time for the planes to be returning, David got off the tractor and walked to the house. It was nearly 4:00 p.m., tea time, and even Grandfather took a break for that.

"If you and Mary can get to the airfield and back in time to milk, you can check on Tex and the crew," Grandfather offered.

"Oh, thank you," David and Mary said in unison.

"And while you're there, invite them to a celebration dinner day after tomorrow," Nana added.

Nana's confidence in the crew's safe return made

David feel better. He hoped it was justified. He and Mary gulped their tea and left quickly.

"Crikey, how much do you weigh?" David groaned as he stood up while pumping with Mary riding on the bicycle seat.

"Not much. You must have weak legs," she retorted.

It took longer than usual to get to Hethel. David heard returning bombers thundering overhead. Sweating, he pedaled faster. He wished he could watch the sky.

"What do you see?" he asked Mary.

"Gaps in the formation," she reported to him, her voice trembly.

As they got nearer, Mary cheered, "I see the *Pat!* She must have come in first. She's smoking, but she made it."

By the time David and Mary pulled up to the hedge and jumped off the bike, the Pat was lumbering up to the hardstand. David could see flak holes gaping in several places.

The ground crew was whooping and holding fingers up in the victory sign as the *Pat* came to a stop. David and Mary jumped the hedge and joined them, overjoyed. David looked up at the cockpit side window

where he usually saw Tex sitting. The window was shattered. Tex wasn't there. Whatever had hit that window must have hit him, David felt sure.

Worried, he watched each exhausted crewman jump to the ground. They clapped waiting ground crew members on the back and headed to the waiting truck. Tex was the last one out.

"Tex!" he cried in alarm. Tex's leather jacket was covered with blood. His head was wrapped in a blood-soaked bandage. Cuts slashed across his face.

CHAPTER 20

In spite of his wounds, Tex smiled. He shook Pop's hand with both of his, then turned and grinned at Mary and David.

"Piece of flak shattered my window and grazed my head—close call!" he explained, pointing to the scarf bandage. "Just need a few stitches."

He grabbed Mary and hugged her hard. She blushed and blinked back tears. Then he turned to David, laid a hand on his shoulder, and walked him around the plane one last time. "Thank God, David, we made it! We're goin' home!" He threw his head back and whooped loudly. Then he laughed, and it reminded David of his father.

Two days later, the crew came to a noisy and excited celebration with David's family. When it was time to say goodbye, the men gave the family hearty handshakes and headed out the door. Tex lingered behind. He shook hands with Grandfather and hugged Nana and Mum, then turned and bear-hugged David. Smelling the familiar leather of Tex's flight jacket, David fought down the lump in his throat. His friend and hero was leaving. It felt as if all happiness were draining out of his life. He glanced at Mary's sorrowful face and knew she must be thinking the same thing. What would they do without him?

"I'll write," Tex said, with a smile that looked a little lopsided with emotion. "You write me and let me know how the *Pat* and Pop are gettin' along, O.K.?"

"O.K.," David said, trying to smile back.

Nana steered the family out of the room while Tex told Mary goodbye. David looked back long enough to see her melt into his arms.

When Tex was gone, even though he had letters to look forward to, David felt a gaping hole in his life—a hole that seemed to intensify his longing for his father. He still spent time with Pop and the chaplain. He still loved the planes. But, a strange, persistent loneliness plagued him.

Over the fall and winter of 1944, David met some new

American friends. He helped pass out candy and gifts at the Yanks' Christmas party for the village children. When he could, he met the *Pat* when she returned from a mission, even though the new crew rushed to debriefings and didn't pay much attention to him. The *Pat's* safe return meant more to him than just something to write to Tex about. Somehow the plane's survival gave him hope that his father was surviving, too.

He turned 15 and celebrated the New Year of 1945 with his family. By mid-January, things were really looking up. The Allies were taking back Europe. Hitler was on the run. By spring, everyone believed Hitler's surrender would come very soon, even though Lord Haw Haw continued to bluster about more secret weapons to come. There were new V-2 rocket bombs, a quiet, more deadly version of the V-1, but David knew Haw Haw and the Germans were getting desperate.

As David carved more Spitfires for the toy store, he thought about his father. Had he survived? Was he a prisoner of war? Or was he part of the Underground and able to help those fighters against Germany?

David's family probably wouldn't know until the war ended, and after that, he didn't know how long it would take to find out.

On May 7, Grandfather's birthday, David woke with a slight sore throat and headache. When he complained, Nana felt his forehead.

"You've got a bit of fever, lad," she said. "Better not milk today. Mary can take your place. Go back to bed. You can make up your school work later."

He gladly crawled back into bed, head pounding, and went to sleep. He was so tired.

He awoke to church bells ringing. He sat up. This was Monday, wasn't it?

Getting out of bed and feeling a little better, he walked into the living room just as Mary, Nana and Grandfather turned from the radio and erupted in cheers. Even Grandfather whooped. "It's over! The war is over!" Mary shouted to David. She began to cry joyful tears. "Thank God! We've won! It's over!"

David's mind couldn't quite take it in. The war was really over? Grandfather scooped up Nana, Mary hugged David, and then he, too, began shouting, "It's over! We won! Dad can come home!" He was determined to believe it.

They listened to Churchill's address that afternoon. "We have never seen a greater day than this," Churchill concluded. "Long live the cause of freedom."

That evening, after his mother had returned from work and chores were done, David decided to ride into Norwich with the family. Grandfather's using the rationed petrol to ride in the car was an event in itself.

"Do you feel up to it?" his mother asked David.

"I think the news has cured me," David said. He really did feel better.

As they drove to Norwich, Grandfather picked up as many walking neighbors as could squeeze into the car. Entering the city, David laughed, "Street lights! Look at 'em!" He hadn't seen them on for six long years.

They drove to the marketplace, where everyone piled out of the car and into the whistling, cheering, gleeful crowd. It was a teeming sea of civilians, soldiers, sailors and airmen, many standing on lampposts. As bands played, people danced, including Scottish soldiers in swirling kilts. Someone started singing the "Conga" song. At the top of their voices others joined in, "I ya, I ya, Conga. I ya, I ya, Conga!" Grabbing each other's waists, making a long snake of dancers, they wound through the crowd, dancing past bombed-out buildings and rubble piles. David felt himself grinning so much that his cheeks hurt.

Shops were lit. Church bells pealed. Searchlights, rigged up by the Army, shone on City Hall and the 900-year-old cathedral, which had miraculously survived the bombing. Other searchlights continually swept the skies, illuminating American and RAF planes that flew over with all their lights on, dropping colored flares.

"I'd forgotten how beautiful lights are," Mary said. "And imagine how excited the little ones are; they've never seen lights at night." Laughing children ran along the pavement holding colorful Union Jacks that flapped in the wind. The world seemed deliriously joyful and relieved.

Later, they went to thanksgiving services at church, gratefully singing hymns in the echoing sanctuary. Then they returned home to listen to a repeat of the King's speech on the radio. David could hear the crowd of thousands in London who had stood in the streets cheering.

"This has been a great day," David sighed contentedly, as Grandfather turned off the radio. "But it'll be even greater when Dad comes home." He made sure he didn't say the word "if."

The war wasn't entirely over. Not only were his father and many others missing, but many in the Royal Norfolk Regiment were prisoners of the Japanese in the Far East. The Allies had to defeat Japan now. But at least, he thought, there were no blackout curtains to draw tonight. And he felt so exhausted, he was glad he didn't have to draw them.

When he went to bed, still with a slight headache, he lay there a long time, listening to the strange quiet. The skies were silent for the first time in nearly six years.

If his dad were alive, he wondered, did he know the Allies had won?

CHAPTER 21

"**G**randfather, since today's a public holiday, I'm sure there's no school," David said after milking the next morning. "May I go into Norwich if I'm back by the evening milking?"

"For someone who was sick just yesterday, you've made a speedy recovery," Grandfather said. Then unexpectedly, he smiled. "Go celebrate, lad. Do some of it for me."

"Thanks." David couldn't believe it.

Then his grandfather added, "But check and see when school will start again."

David, Roger and Mac went to street parties celebrating Victory in Europe Day with games and food and dancing. David looked hungrily at the sweets set out on long tables—chocolate cake, sponge cakes, lemonade, chocolate biscuits, toffee apples, ice cream. He'd almost forgotten what they tasted like, but soon found out.

"Where did all the sugar come from?" David asked, licking chocolate frosting from his fingers.

"People must have been saving it, waiting for this day," Roger said. "And now Mac is hoarding as much as he can in his cheeks."

David looked at Mac, whose cheeks were bulging with cake, and laughed.

They cycled all over the city, and then to Wroxham Broad where many Americans were celebrating on houseboats. They were invited to join in the fun.

As much as David enjoyed the day, thoughts of his father plagued him. Somehow, celebrating began to feel hollow. David left his friends to return home in time for tea. As he rode down the lane, the silent skies made him feel lonely.

Mary was whistling in the kitchen, putting the kettle on, when he came in.

"How was Norwich?" she asked.

"Super. But, I began thinking about Dad again, and the fun went out of it."

"I know," Mary said. "But listen. I have a secret that might cheer you up. You can't tell anyone."

"What?"

"Six months after the war in Japan is over, Tex will be finished with the military. And he's asked me to marry him! I said yes."

"Jeepers!" David whooped. Tex would be in the family! Then reality seized him. "But you'd have to move 4,000 miles away."

"We'll visit. You can come to Texas and spend summers at the ranch."

David hardly listened. "But what'll Mum say? What if Dad doesn't come home?" David sat down at the table. "If you leave, it'd be too much for Mum."

"What would?" Grandfather interrupted, coming in.

"If we don't hear about Dad soon," Mary said quickly. "Some people in the village have already heard; the Smith's son, who was missing in action, just appeared at their door yesterday. Can you imagine?"

David thought Mary was smart to keep her secret and change the subject. He wondered what Grandfather's reaction would be if he knew the whole truth.

"That is wonderful news about the Smith lad!" Grandfather smiled, joining David at the table. "He'll get to march in Sunday's parade in Norwich. What a proud moment for his whole family."

"There's going to be a parade?" David asked.

"Yes, with all Britain's armed forces, the Yanks, our other Allies and all the voluntary services. So you two will march in it, too—Mary with the Land Army, and you with your Scout troop, David. Make sure your uniform is clean."

"Super!" David exclaimed, adding, "I just wish ..."

"We'll go in Dad's honor," Mary finished for him, setting the tea on the table. "And we'll tell him about it when he comes home."

Parade Sunday was gray and cloudy, but nothing dampened the mood of the throngs of people lining the streets of Norwich. David, Roger and Mac marched in their Scout group behind the troops, caught up in the excitement of the cheers. Spectators were crammed so closely together that some took to the rooftops where they waved and clapped. Military bands led the way from the City Hall through the city to the Cathedral for a thanksgiving service. In crisp uniforms, in perfect step, looking straight ahead were the heroes—the Army, Navy, Royal Air Force, the Yanks and troops of many nationalities. Flags snapped in the moist breeze. In the long stream of people, David had no idea where Mary was. He felt proud and happy, yet sad, too, because his main hero, his dad, was missing.

After the festivities, the days dragged by while David and his family waited in vain for news of his father. Exams were nearing, so one Saturday David pedaled out to Hethel for his last laundry run until school was over.

"Grandfather's making me stay home and study for the next 10 days," he complained to Pop and Chaplain. "Says I need to concentrate. Mary's getting the laundry run. What a mess!"

"Your grandfather is right. Better study," Pop said. "You still want to be a pilot, right?"

"Yes."

"Well then, work hard and don't worry about us," Pop said with a grin. "We'll be leaving sometime soon, but we'll look for you after exams."

"I'll pray for you," Chaplain added.

"Thanks." David smiled. "See you when school's out."

David thought it was like punishment to sit through long school days, then spend all his spare time studying. In his room, he stared at his model airplanes and the bomb fragments he'd collected and tried to memorize his school notes. He couldn't wait to get back to the airfield when exams were over.

"Blast!" David griped to Roger the day before school let out. "All Grandfather can think about is my marks! I hope the Yanks don't leave before we get out of school."

"Let's ride out to Hethel first thing tomorrow when we're finished," Roger suggested.

The next day, the three friends took off as quickly as they could, with Mac jabbering the whole way. But Mac was shocked into sudden silence. David quickly saw why. He couldn't believe his eyes. Every plane was gone. There was no guard at the main gate. It was empty. Eerily silent.

"Let's go in," Mac said.

"Maybe someone is left in the barracks," David agreed, hopefully. Maybe at least Chaplain would be there.

They parked their bicycles and wandered through the

huts. Empty! They walked through Chaplain's hut, finding a copy of *Yank* still on the desk. The mess hall where they'd enjoyed so many treats was deserted. So was the tower.

"Can you believe everybody's gone? Just like that?" Roger asked.

David shook his head sadly. Then his eye caught something. "Look!" he exclaimed, running to collect a steel helmet left beside a hangar.

"I wish I'd found that," Mac lamented.

"I'll race you for it," David said. "Let's ride on the runway."

He put the helmet on. The boys flew down the main runway. As the wind blew in his face, David pumped hard, wishing he could pedal away the deep sadness of not saying goodbye.

He won the race, but he gave the helmet to Mac anyway. He couldn't tell them his secret about Tex, but he knew Mac needed a remembrance more than he did.

The boys rode home, Mac exclaiming the whole way about the smashing time they'd had and how much he liked the helmet. But David was heavy-hearted.

As they split up to go their separate ways, David felt that familiar, aching loneliness growing stronger. It seemed it would overwhelm him, and he pedaled harder, hoping somehow to outrun it.

Like a storm cloud in his mind, it triggered flashes of frightening possibilities. What if the reason they hadn't heard about his dad was because he was dead and no one had found him? What if the tragic news made Grandfather bitter and harder to live with than ever, and then Mary moved to America? Would he and Mum move back to London? What if Mum lost her spirit, and David couldn't measure up to being "the man of the house" his father had expected him to be?

The future suddenly seemed almost as frightening as the war had been. David tried to summon up the hope and courage he'd felt in the days after the fire rescue and the thrilling announcement of Victory in Europe Day. Where had the optimism gone?

Turning onto the lane leading to the farmhouse, he looked down the hill at Attlebridge's runways criss-crossing the fields where his father had worked as a boy. Planes still flew from there, taking food, water and medical supplies to hungry war victims in Holland and Belgium, victims who would rebuild their lives amid the rubble that had been Europe. The Brits were doing the same. So much of England had been destroyed. Yet they had survived, for six long years. They'd made it.

He couldn't give up now, no matter what happened. "Set your mind to it," he reminded himself, quoting his grandfather aloud. After all, he was part of a race of brave, stubborn people who would never give up. In spite of his doubts about himself, he had their blood in his veins. His father's blood. And if he could pull a man from a burning house, then with God's help, he could become the man his dad wanted him to be. He felt his confidence returning. His spirits lifted.

As he stared at the airfield and on down the road, he saw a solitary figure walking toward the house from the field. The form looked familiar. Grandfather? What had he been doing at Attlebridge? He watched the limping gait. Something was different. The man didn't walk like Grandfather, but more like a younger man. Like …

"Father!" he screamed, tearing down the hill on his bike. "Dad!" The figure stopped, turned. As David flew

toward him, the figure began to limp faster, half running. The face was clearer now, the beloved face, eyes and smile wide with gladness.

"Dad!" His bike skidding to a halt, and with his eyes brimming with tears, David jumped off the bicycle. He threw his arms around his father's thin frame, nearly toppling him.

"David!" His father's voice was husky as his arms crushed him in an embrace. "David, you've grown up!"

Suddenly shouts and squeals rang out as the whole family poured from the house, running toward them. In seconds, six bodies crushed together in a tight squeeze. Tears streamed down every face—even Grandfather's. David felt as if he were in the middle of a dream. He'd never felt such joy.

In all the commotion, one distinct sound rang out. It was the sound David had prayed to hear again someday—his father's hearty laugh. And caught in the middle of happy hugs and tears, David laughed, too.

EPILOGUE

T he story of the fictitious character David Freeman is based on the life of two people, David Hastings and the late Roger Freeman, both of whom, as children and adults, had special bonds of friendship with members of the Eighth Air Force. Although a few of the boy David's experiences are fictitious, most of the story's happenings are true, taken from the two men's lives plus those of several others who were children in England during World War II.

Roger Freeman's boyhood experiences grew into a lifelong occupation. Growing up on a farm in the small village of Dedham, England, he became a farmer and a well-known historian of the Eighth Air Force. He authored more than 60 books, including *The Mighty Eighth*. He coined the term *Mighty Eighth* to describe the men and machines of the Eighth Air Force. All his life, Roger kept the aviation notebooks from his boyhood that had gotten him into trouble with the RAF security police. He led seminars throughout the world teaching about the people and events of that "unique period of history." He met David Hastings as an adult, and they served together as Trust Governors of the Memorial Library in Norwich, which was set up by the 2nd Air Division of the USAAF to honor their fallen comrades.

David Hastings, who still has the quarter the American airman gave him as well as his wartime notebook, grew up in Norwich, England, and still lives there. As a young man, he joined the Royal Air Force as a National Serviceman. In the RAF Transport Command, he served in Germany during reconstruction of that country. He said, "It seemed odd to be part of the crew flying food and coal for people who only a few years back had tried to kill me and my parents in the Blitz."

After his service in the RAF, David Hastings became a pilot. He searched nearly 40 years to find his childhood hero and close friend in the war, Lt. Al Dexter. Finally, in 1990, Lt. Dexter and his family visited England, and the two were reunited. Together they stood on the site where they first met in 1944. They gave thanks for their reunion and friendship in the ruins of the base chapel there.

In 1992, David's childhood dream of flying a Liberator became a reality. As part of the celebration of the 50th anniversary of the Mighty Eighth's arrival in Great Britain, he helped arrange Britain's portion of a tour of a famous B-24 named *Diamond Lil*. Because of his efforts, he was appointed a Colonel in the Commemorative Air Force and helped to fly the 51-year-old *Diamond Lil* across the Atlantic to England. He met Al Dexter in Norwich, and together they took off from Horsham St. Faith and flew over the countryside.

"There we were, the wartime pilot and the young English schoolboy, reunited in a free world, flying in a Liberator, but this time as two pilots," David recalls.

He works tirelessly as a governor of the 2nd Air Division USAAF Memorial Library Trust in Norwich. This unique library honors the 7,000 young Americans of that division of the Eighth Air Force who died flying from Britain's airfields. Of the surviving men of the Mighty Eighth, David says, "They came as friends, they stayed as friends, they have remained friends. We and future generations will always remember them with pride and affection."

• • •

MIGHTY EIGHTH AIR FORCE MUSEUM (USA)

You can learn more about the Eighth Air Force by visiting the Mighty Eighth Air Force Museum near Savannah, Georgia (USA), or by visiting their website at www.mightyeighth.org.

The Museum first opened its doors in May 1996, making history come alive for young and old alike. It was the realization of a plan envisioned by B-17 bomber pilot Major Gen. Lewis E. Lyle and other veterans. They wanted to honor the men and women who helped defeat Nazi aggression by serving in or supporting the greatest air armada the world had ever seen—the

Eighth Air Force. With its many exhibits, the museum honors the courage, sacrifice and patriotism of those who fought for freedom. Flying from bases in East Anglia, England, more than 56,000 8th Air Force airmen were shot down by the German enemy during WWII. (Over 28,000 became prisoners of war, about 47,000 were wounded, more than 26,000 died.)

The Museum has become the home for thousands of artifacts, personal effects, books, art and amazing stories of wartime heroism and valor. Adding continually to its growing collections of vintage aircraft, theatre presentations and interactive exhibits, the Mighty Eighth Air Force Museum combines state-of-the art technology with artifacts, entertaining and educating more than 120,000 annual visitors, including 15,000 students.

The Roger A. Freeman Eighth Air Force Research Center houses archival manuscript and photographic collections, as well as artifacts and rare books of Eighth Air Force history. Library staff assists visitors worldwide in gathering information and providing research assistance. The museum preserves the stories of courage, character and patriotism embodied by the men and women of the Eighth Air Force, from World War II to the present, treasuring and teaching these values for all generations.

Mighty Eighth Air Force Museum
P.O. Box 1992
Savannah, Ga. 31402
912-748-8888
www.mightyeighth.org

2ⁿᵈ AIR DIVISION USAAF MEMORIAL LIBRARY
(England)

In Norwich, England, you can visit the 2ⁿᵈ Air Division's Memorial Library to experience some of their history. Inside are a large mural and drawings of aircraft from each of the 14 Bomb Groups, a large-scale model of a B-24 Liberator, and models of each Bomb Group's "Assembly Ships," which helped the bombers to safely gather in their own formations in the murky morning skies over England. The library also has a B-24 flight simulator, the first of its kind in the world, on which visitors to the Library are able to participate in virtual reality flights.

The idea for a Norwich memorial began early in 1945, even before the hostilities in Europe were over. Men of the 2nd Air Division wanted to establish a memorial in East Anglia to honor their fallen comrades (just under 7,000 died in their air division) and also honor the survivors of the fight for freedom. Because of post-war shortages, however, the library was not built until 1963. A fire destroyed the original building in 1994.

Today, a stately and beautiful hall of memory in Norwich, twice as big as the first building, contains a "living memorial library," which has video and oral history collections and houses the 2nd Air Division's Roll of Honour (those who lost their lives), Book of Remembrance and the Division's Standards. It also has an extensive range of books covering all aspects of American life and history, and houses the 2nd Air Division archives and the unique Dzenowagis videotape collection. This memorial, the only one of its kind in the world, has become a treasured part of Norfolk life and a focal point for all occasions when the 2nd Air Division Association returns to Norwich for their conventions. The Library also provides details as to how to reach all the old 2nd Air Division airfields.

The Memorial Library is housed in the Millennium Building, known as The Forum, which also includes the Central Library, The Origins Heritage Visitor Attraction Centre, Tourist Information and Visitor Centre, Learning Shop, restaurant, and BBC radio and television studios.

The 2nd Air Division USAAF Memorial Library
The Forum, Millennium Plain
Norwich, Norfolk, NR2 1AW, England
Tel: 01603-774747
Web site address: www.2ndair.org.uk
Email: 2admemorial.lib@norfolk.gov.uk
Web site address: www.2ndair.org.uk

IMPERIAL WAR MUSEUM WEB SITE

The Imperial War Museum, the multi-branch national museum of war and wartime life from the First World War through the Second World War, offers information at their website. For London's museum, check out London.iwm.org.uk/. At Duxford, try duxford.iwm.org.uk/.

TIMELINE

1939:

September 1—Germany invades Poland; World War II begins.

September 27—Poland surrenders to Germany.

1940:

April 9—Germany invades Denmark and Norway.

May 10—Germany invades Luxembourg, Holland and Belgium.

May 26–June 4—British Expeditionary Force is evacuated from Dunkirk, France.

June 10—Italy declares war on Britain and France.

June 22—France signs an armistice with Germany, becoming an occupied country.

July 10-October 31—Battle of Britain: Royal Air Force holds off a German invasion of England.

1941:

June 22—Germany invades the Soviet Union.

December 7—Japan attacks Pearl Harbor (Hawaii).

December 8—Japan declares war on United States and Britain.

December 11—Germany and Italy declare war on the United States.

1942:

June 25—Gen. Dwight D. Eisenhower assumes command of all U.S. troops in Europe.

November 8—American and British troops land in French North Africa in order to secure bases for future operations. The battle for North Africa lasts until May 1943.

1943:

April 23—Anglo-American headquarters are established in Britain to plan invasion of Europe.

December 24—General Eisenhower is named Supreme Allied Commander for the invasion of Western Europe.

1944:

January–May—Soviets begin retaking their country from the Germans.

June 4—The first Axis capital falls, as the Allies liberate Rome, Italy.

June 6—D-Day: Allies land in Normandy, France.

June–December—Allies battle for supremacy.

1945:

January 19—Germans are in full retreat along eastern front.

April 12—American President Roosevelt dies; Harry S. Truman becomes president.

April 16–May 2—Battle of Berlin (German capital)

April 29—German forces surrender in Italy.

April 30—Hitler commits suicide in Berlin.

May 7—Germany formally surrenders.

May 8—Victory in Europe Day

August 6—An American B-29 bomber, the *Enola Gay,* drops the first atomic bomb used in warfare on the Japanese city of Hiroshima. A second bomb is dropped on Nagasaki on August 9.

September 2—Japan surrenders. Representatives of all the Allied nations are present for the signing of the surrender on the U.S. battleship *Missouri.* President Truman declares Victory in Japan Day, and World War II is finally ended.

(The work consulted for this timeline: *Strategic Battles in Europe* by Earle Rice, Jr., and *World Book Encyclopedia.*)

GLOSSARY

Aeroplane: English spelling of airplane

Air Crew: men who worked as a team on flying missions, including the pilot, co-pilot, navigator, bombardier, radio operator, flight engineers, and gunners

Allies: the countries that fought together against the Axis powers in WWII, the major ones being Great Britain, the Soviet Union, China and the United States. (The Allies totaled 50 nations by the end of the war.)

Axis: the name used to describe the countries of Germany, Japan and Italy, which united against the Allies (Six other nations eventually joined the Axis.)

Blitzkrieg (Blitz): a very powerful and quick (like "lightning") war

East Anglia: the region of Great Britain where most of the military airfields were built that were used by the Eighth Air Force and other Allied forces flying over Europe

Flak: anti-aircraft gunfire (the word took its letters from the German word flugabwehkanone)

Ground Crew: personnel who worked on the ground around-the-clock readying each airplane for the next mission. To keep the airplanes in good running order, a crew chief was assigned to each plane to be in charge, as he and three other men repaired planes, checked instruments, replaced parts, installed fresh oxygen tanks, checked guns, restocked ammunition and bombs, refueled planes and performed many other maintenance jobs.

Hardstand: the concrete area where an airplane was parked

Luftwaffe: German Air Force formed in 1935. In the war years, more than 3.4 million served in the Luftwaffe (more than 300,000 were killed or missing; more than 192,000 were wounded).

MP: Military Police

Nazi: a member of the German National Socialist Party and militant follower of Adolf Hitler

Occupied Country: a country under the enemy's military possession or control

Propaganda: an organized program of publicity used to spread ideas and false information

Pearl Harbor: an American naval base at Honolulu, Hawaii, attacked by Japan on December 7, 1941

POW: Prisoner of War

RAF: Royal Air Force

Rationing: a system of requiring coupons for the purchase of food, clothing and other scarce items so that everyone had an equal share

VE Day: Victory in Europe Day

VJ Day: Victory in Japan Day

V-Weapon (such as V-1 bomb or V-2 rocket): the abbreviation for vengeance weapon. The German word was Vergeltunswaffen.

Air Crew Positions:

Pilot and Co-pilot: officers who flew the plane (One other crew member was unofficially trained to land the plane in case both pilots were badly injured.)

Navigator: officer who plotted the course to the target

Bombardier (or Bomb aimer in the RAF): officer responsible for the aiming and release of bombs. Later in the war, the bombardier was replaced by a togglier in any planes that were not flying lead in a formation. This was because the planes following the lead plane all dropped their bombs when the lead plane did.

Radio (wireless) Operator: responsible for all radio communication and radio navigation aids (who also acted as a gunner)

Flight Engineer: responsible for engines and fuel systems; also served as top turret gunner

Gunners: manned various gun positions, wearing electrically-heated flying suits, gloves and boots to protect from subzero cold. They were the following:

Tail Gunner sat in the rear of the bomber, facing backward, to defend against enemy fighters in pursuit.

Left and Right Waist Gunners defended their aircraft from fighters on either side.

Nose Turret Gunner defended from front of plane.

Top Turret Gunner fired from the top of the plane. (Often this position was filled by the flight engineer.)

Ball Turret Gunner sat in a swiveling plexiglas ball underneath belly of plane. The ball turret was taken out later in the war to increase plane speed and reduce weight.

W O R L D   W A R   I I   A I R P L A N E S

United States:

Fighters

  Republican P-47 Thunderbolt

    Armament: 8 .50-cal machine guns (MGs)

                  1,500 lbs. of bombs or 10 rockets

    Speed: 440 mph

    Ceiling: 40,000 ft.

    Range: 800 miles (internal tanks)

  North American P-51 Mustang

    Armament: 6 .50-cal MGs; up to 2,000 lbs. of bombs

    Speed: 445 mph

    Ceiling: 40,000 ft.

    Range: 1,000 miles (internal tanks)

Bombers

  Boeing B-17 Flying Fortress

    Armament: 13 .50-cal MGs; up to 6,000 lbs. of bombs

    Speed: 295 mph

    Ceiling: 35,000 ft.

    Range: 1,100 miles (internal tanks)

    Crew Size: 10

Consolidated B-24 Liberator

Armament: 10 .50-cal MGs; up to 8,000 lbs. of bombs

Speed: 297 mph

Ceiling: 28,000 ft.

Range: 1,540 miles (internal tanks)

Crew Size: 8–10

England:

Fighters

Hawker Hurricane

Armament: Varied—.303-cal MGs and 20-mm cannon

Speed: 340 mph

Ceiling: 41,000 ft.

Range: 600 miles (internal tanks)

Supermarine Spitfire

Armament: 2 20-mm cannons and 4 .303-cal MGs

Speed: 422 mph

Ceiling: 45,000 ft.

Range: 640 miles (internal tanks)

Bombers

Avro Lancaster

Armament: 10 .303-cal MGs; up to 16,000 lbs. of bombs or 1 22,000-lb. bomb

Speed: 275 mph

Ceiling: 23,500 ft.

Range: 3,000 miles (internal tanks)

Crew Size: 7

Wellington (Vickers Wellington MK I)

Armament: 6 MGs; 4,500 lbs. of bombs

Speed: 235 mph at 15,500 ft.

Ceiling: 18,000 ft.

Range: 2,200 miles

Crew Size 6

Halifax (Handley Page Halifax MK I)

Armament: 6 MGs; 13,000 lbs. of bombs

Speed: 265 mph at 17,500 ft

Ceiling: 22,800 ft.

Range: 1,860 miles

Crew: 7

Halifax (Handley Page Halifax MK III)

Armament: 9 MGs; 13,000 lbs. of bombs

Speed: 282 mph at 13,500 ft

Ceiling: 20,000 ft.

Range: 1,077 miles

Crew: 7

GERMANY

Fighters

Focke Wulf Fw-190

Armament: 4 20-mm cannons

Speed: 402 mph

Ceiling: 37,400 ft.

Range: 950 miles

Messerschmitt Bf 109 (Me-109)

Armament: 2 13-mm cannons and 3 20-mm cannons

Speed 428 mph

Ceiling: 20,000 ft.

Range: 350 miles (internal tanks)

AIRFIELDS OF THE EIGHTH AIR FORCE 1942-1945

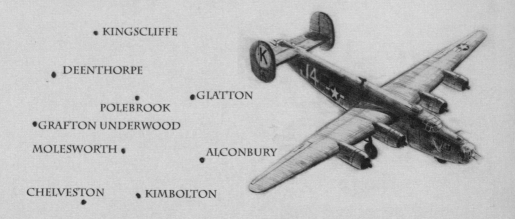

- KINGSCLIFFE
- DEENTHORPE
- POLEBROOK
- GLATTON
- GRAFTON UNDERWOOD
- MOLESWORTH
- ALCONBURY
- CHELVESTON
- KIMBOLTON
- THURLEIGH
- PODINGTON
- BOTTISHAM
- BASSINGBOURN
- DUXFORD
- STEEPLE MORDEN
- FOWLMERE
- LITTLE WALDEN
- RIDGEWELL
- NUTHAMPSTEAD
- DEBDEN
- EARLS COLNE
- ANDREWS FIELD
- GREAT DUNMOW

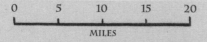

0   5   10   15   20

MILES